She knew she would never be the same

Katriona held Morgan's letter close, keeping it, holding it, treasuring it. Something of his.

She felt her cheeks burn as she realized where her thoughts were leading. What if Morgan had made love to her? Pain shot through her as Katriona forced herself to be honest and admit she would have been wild with delight. Morgan Grant had some powerful magical quality that drew people to him. Look how Jeannie and Donald had been charmed, and Elspeth, and silly, stupid, idiotic Katriona Carmichael!

Katriona caught her reflection in the mirror, and it did not look like her at all. The girl in the mirror had a soft, sweet mouth, color in her cheeks and stars in her eyes.

She looked like a girl in love!

Man of the High Country

by

MARY MOORE

Harlequin Books

TORONTO·LONDON·NEW YORK·AMSTERDAM
SYDNEY·HAMBURG·PARIS·STOCKHOLM

Original hardcover edition published in 1979
by Mills & Boon Limited

ISBN 0-373-02349-9

Harlequin edition published August 1980

Printed in U.S.A.

CHAPTER ONE

KATRIONA CARMICHAEL was typing furiously fast, her whole concentration centred on finishing these last three very long complicated letters for her employer, Mr Drummond. She was so deeply engrossed in her work that she failed to hear the knock on her door or see the little office junior peer cautiously round the door and tiptoe up to her desk.

'Miss Carmichael. Please, Miss Carmichael.' Shona's face was flushed with excitement. She had to get Katriona's attention somehow. Determinedly she raised her voice and shouted, *'Katriona!'*

Katriona looked up, 'Yes, Shona, what is it? Sorry I didn't see you there.'

Looking somewhat embarrassed, Shona blurted out, 'It's that man again, asking for you. Won't you please see him? He's awfully nice, really he is . . . and he says he has to see you most urgently. I know you're very busy, but it would only take a few minutes.'

Anger flashed in Katriona's blue eyes. 'Now, Shona, I told you yesterday, and again this morning, that I don't want to see him. That's *final*. This is my last day at work before I go on holiday, and I have simply masses of stuff to get through for Mr Drummond. Now, go out and tell him to get lost—politely of course, but firmly.' Katriona returned to her typing.

Rather nervously Shona stood her ground. Miss Carmichael, the private secretary of the president of the Company, could be a bit scary when she got angry, but Shona felt the man at the public counter might also be a bit difficult if he was put off again.

Katriona ripped the finished letter from her typewriter with a flourish and clipped the original and three copies

together, ready for signing, then put in fresh paper and
carbons. 'One down, two to go,' she muttered. Then she
saw Shona still standing beside her desk, and raised one
eyebrow questioningly.

'Oh, Miss Carmichael, don't get mad. I can't go back and
tell Mr Grant you won't see him. He won't believe me,
and it's embarrassing. This is the fourth time he's been
here, and he must know you're avoiding him.'

'I should hope he does by now,' Katriona replied briskly.
'It will save him wasting his time, your time, and my time.'

Shona still hovered. 'I know you said he was one of your
mother's A.Y.M. people, whatever they are ... but he
doesn't look peculiar. He looks nice, and serious ...'

Katriona sighed impatiently. 'They often do. Mother
sends them over here to Edinburgh with strict instructions
to see her "dear wee girl" and show her a good time, and in
that way she eases her conscience for her neglect of her
only daughter. A.Y.M. means Aimless Young Man or
Awful Young Man. You could quite well use any vowel in
the alphabet to describe them, for example, E.Y.M., Earnest
Y.M., or Incredible Y.M., or Obnoxious Y.M., or Useless
Y.M. They're all cut to the same pattern, too much money
... oh, it's no use trying to explain it to you again. Just go
out and get rid of him. Is that clear?'

Shona nodded despondently. She watched Katriona slip
the paper into place and start typing another letter. She
knew it was useless to argue further, but it was always a
pleasure to watch Katriona at work, and it postponed having to disappoint that nice-looking man at the public
counter. Idly she daydreamed of the day she would be
as competent and efficient at Katriona, friendly towards
everyone yet sort of reserved, keeping herself to herself. Of
course, Katriona was fabulous to look at with that glorious
shoulder-length red hair and blue, blue eyes, and when she
batted those fantastically long sweeping eyelashes ...

Katriona glanced up and caught Shona's admiring gaze
and jerked her head towards the door significantly. Shona
left the room hurriedly.

An hour later when Shona appeared with Katriona's afternoon tea on a tray, she found the secretary relaxed and busy tidying her desk. 'Thank you, Shona. Sorry I bit your head off last time, but those letters were very important.'

Shona shrugged her shoulders. 'It didn't bother me, Miss Carmichael.'

'Nice child,' Katriona commented as she sipped her tea with appreciation. 'Everything is cleared up here and I'm off as soon as I finish this. I'm looking forward to two wonderful weeks' leave before the tourist rush begins.'

'You're leaving early?' Shona asked in shocked tones. Miss Carmichael never left early. She always checked the windows and doors and safe before leaving.

Katriona did not notice Shona's dismay. 'Yes, Mr Drummond said to take an earlier train to Glasgow, and that suits me fine. I love the train trip from Glasgow to Oban in June when all the bluebells are in flower among the trees, and the red splashes of colour from the rhododendrons are everywhere. I'll sleep on the ferry, and be on Tiree next morning.'

'But you can't,' wailed Shona. 'I told Mr Grant he should be here when the office closed, if he wanted to see you so badly.'

Katriona chuckled. 'Oh, Shona, he's not going to be very pleased with you, is he? Serve him right for being so persistent.'

'Honestly, Miss Carmichael, you'd like him if you met him. Won't you stay and see him, *please*?'

'No,' Katriona replied firmly. 'I'm off on holiday, and by the time I return Mr Grant will have taken himself off to Paris or Rome or wherever. Don't feel too badly about it, dear. He'll probably feel terribly relieved, even though he'll make a great show of being bitterly disappointed. Just bear in mind that it is a show and you won't feel too guilty.'

'I'm sure he's genuine,' Shona protested.

'Oh, he will be genuinely sorry that he can't do the favour my mother asked him to do. Most men find it impossible to refuse her anything. She has quite a way with her.'

Shona heard the tinge of bitterness in Katriona's voice, and was puzzled. 'But why does your mother keep sending these men? She must know you're so lovely you only have to lift a finger and you could have any young man you wanted.'

Katriona laughed, 'Shona, my dear, you're a definite asset to the office, a real ego-builder!' A sudden thought struck her. 'You didn't tell him I was going on holiday?—Mr Grant, I mean?'

Shona shook her head despondently.

'Good,' Katriona said forcefully. 'And you won't. If he appears next week you'll be quite vague as to where I've gone or when I'm coming back. Do you understand?'

'Yes,' Shona answered unhappily. Miss Carmichael might brush her visitor aside as insignificant, but she, Shona, could not see him tamely accepting defeat. Romantically, she could see him flying off to that wee island where Miss Carmichael was staying—but now she couldn't even give him any information to help him get there. 'He's really a dish,' she offered hopefully.

'That's fine,' Katriona told her with a mischievous grin. 'I'm sure you'll enjoy making it up to him for his crushing disappointment.'

Shona watched Katriona finish her tea, then pick up her bag and fling her tartan cloak over her slender shoulders. 'You never do, do you?'

Katriona turned. 'Do what, you funny little thing?'

'You never do lift a finger to encourage any man. You just brush them off. Don't you like men, Miss Carmichael?'

'Oh, I like Mr Drummond, and old Mr Brown, and young William,' Katriona replied flippantly.

For an instant Shona saw something like pain or sadness in those blue eyes, but it flickered and was gone so fast that she began to doubt it had been there. 'But they're really very old or very young. I meant eligible males?'

'Oh, *those*!' Katriona laughed mockingly. 'No. I have to

admit that those sort of men are fine in their place, I'm sure, just as long as they don't feel they have any place in my life. Now I'll say goodbye. See you behave yourself while I'm away.'

Shona picked up the tray still thinking of Katriona Carmichael. She had sounded so hard, yet Shona knew that she was soft-hearted and kind. Perhaps she had been jilted once? No. Shona could not see any man throwing away the chance of being married to the lovely redhead. Perhaps someone she loved very much had died? Yes, that sounded more romantic and fitting. What a pity that she would not meet Mr Grant. Shona was sure that no girl in her right mind would be able to resist Mr Grant.

Katriona caught her train with time to spare, and for the next two weeks blissfully forgot there ever was an office in Edinburgh. As soon as she arrived at the croft, and followed Donald up the narrow stairs as he carried her cases, she shed all her city sophistication. When he left she stripped off her elegant city clothes and scrambled into her sweater and jeans, knowing with joy that here on the island she had no need to project the careful image of the always efficient and cool Miss Carmichael.

But the two weeks flew by on wings, and on her last day she rose early before the sun and climbed to the top of Ben Hynish, the largest of the three hills on Tiree. It gave her a wonderful feeling to be up there alone before any of the Island people stirred from their beds, a feeling of oneness with this wild, lonely, lovely island.

Katriona lay back against the heather on the hill and pushed all the problems from her mind. She watched the huge jets slice through the clear blue Hebridean sky as they arrowed their way to the Scottish International Airport at Prestwick. She thought of the passengers weary from their long journey across the Atlantic soothing their tired eyes on the green fields below, excited by their first glimpse of Scotland. They would be the vanguard of the millions of tourists who would wing their way into Britain for the summer holidays. She envied none of them.

Warmed by the early morning sun, and sheltered from the fresh wind by the heather, she watched a small rock wren warily approach its nest. Alert and watchful, it hopped nearer and nearer to Katriona, then stopped only inches away from her hand and paused long enough to decide that she was only part of the landscape before slipping into a narrow crevice in the rock. Katriona lay scarcely breathing until it re-emerged and flew away. A black-faced Highland ewe with its lamb appeared on the ledge below her and haughtily surveyed the surroundings before giving her a contemptuous glance, then trotted out of sight.

Moving cautiously, Katriona inched forward to look into the tiny nest and with delight she counted four eggs. An amused smile touched her lips and was reflected in her eyes, which were as blue as the Hebridean sky itself. Suddenly conscious of the time, she scrambled to her feet. Yes, folk were stirring down below her. There was Duncan bringing his cows into the byre, and the children playing outside the croft by the loch—Mary Flora, Ishbel, Hector and wee Duncan. Katriona sighed. She must go down. Donald and Jeannie would be expecting her.

She shivered as the chill wind bit through her thick warm sweater, bent hastily to pick up her windbreaker and thankfully slipped her arms into its warmth, then thrust her green tam'-o-shanter on her red-gold curls. Thrusting her hand into the pockets, she felt her fingers curl round a stone and pulled it out to examine it. A pale opalescent green stone, like the Iona stone, heart-shaped, smooth and warm in her palm.

Poor Donald ... no, dear sweet Donald. He had found the stone down on the shore and given it to her, just as he would love to give her his name, his land and anything he owned. Oh, why could she not love him? She knew that she would be happy to spend all her days on this island among the warm hearted folk she knew. Yet all she felt for Donald was friendship, and it wasn't enough. It wasn't enough to offer such a fine man.

Angrily she zipped up her jacket, her peace of mind

shattered and all the old restlessness and yearning back again. She started down the hillside, running and jumping across its craggy slopes, startling the blackfaced sheep and lambs and causing commotion and consternation between the cows and calves grazing on the lower slopes. Down the track she raced and out across the pastures beside the road where she climbed over the gate and breathlessly slowed to a walk as she neared the croft.

'A fine morning to you, Katriona Carmichael,' Donald greeted her as she caught up with him on his way back with the cows.

'And to you, Donald Macdonald,' Katriona returned with a happy smile, stopping to pat the old white cow. 'Fancy calling her the young one, she must feel flattered as she's nearly thirteen years old.'

'It does no harm to flatter the ladies,' Donald told her, his brown eyes laughing down at her. 'No harm at all, at all.'

'You're an awful man, Donald. It's no wonder half the girls on the island would be happy to give Jeannie a rest from housekeeping for you.'

'So they would, no doubt,' Donald grinned at her. 'The trouble being, of course, that I have given my heart to a feckless lassie who lives over the water.'

'Oh, if she's all that feckless,' Katriona retorted, 'I'd give her a miss and settle for someone nearer home.'

Donald held the door open for her. 'I have thought of it, but I'm a patient man and I'm prepared to wait a while longer. She's a bonnie lassie with hair as red as fire and a temper to match, and her eyes are as blue as the bluebells, but not very bright, if you follow me. Sure, she will realise soon what a fine bargain she's missing, and snap me up . . .'

Katriona whirled past him to speak to Jeannie. 'You've got an awfully conceited brother, did you know that, Jeannie?'

Jeannie laughed merrily. 'Of course. How could he be anything else when all the women spoil him so? Now, stop your sparring and wash up. The porridge is ready on the table. I saw you come flying down the hill.'

Later, seated at the table enjoying her breakfast, Katriona felt relaxed and happy. The sun streamed in through the kitchen window and the open door, and borne on the wind was the lilting skirl of the pipes from the croft over the field. 'Young Helen really puts her heart into those pipes.'

'Indeed she does,' Jeannie agreed. 'And she's being taught by Angus himself, who has won more cups than I would care to mention. But it is not your heart or mine that she is hoping to steal away with her piping.' Jeannie slanted a teasing glance at her brother.

Donald rose and pushed back his chair, 'Oh, she knows a fine braw man when she sees one. You'll be coming to church with us, Katriona?'

'Yes, I will.' Katriona laughed impishly. 'I can't resist the thoroughly un-Christian looks I get from the local girls when I walk in on your arm, Donald my love!'

Donald's brown eyes were unusually serious although he spoke lightly. 'Any day that you are willing we will walk down that aisle together, and you can have the permanent satisfaction of knowing you are married to the finest man on the island.'

Catching the troubled expression in Katriona's eyes, Jeannie spoke sharply. 'Away with you, Donald. You're an awful tease. Leave us women to have some talk together.'

As they cleared the dishes and washed them, Jeannie said, 'I wish you were not going away so soon. Your holiday has simply flown by.'

'I know it has,' Katriona agreed sadly. 'I love it here. I do hate to go back to the city. But yourself, Jeannie—aren't you getting impatient to go back to Glasgow? I know you had no choice when Ena died. You had to come home and see to Donald and the house. But that was almost two years ago. Is Bruce not getting angry at all the waiting before you can marry?'

Jeannie had a lovely smile. 'Impatient, yes, you could say that. But he knows I would not be happy if I left Donald to fend for himself. Bruce and I don't have to snatch at our happiness at someone else's cost. We *are* content to wait.

Although it troubles Donald. He has mentioned several times lately that he should get a housekeeper. I know it worries him more than it worries us.'

There was a long silence between them as they tidied up and then sat in the sunshine on the doorstep together.

At last Katriona spoke. 'I can't marry him, Jeannie. I love Donald dearly, but it's the same way that I love you. I'm closer to you two than anyone else on earth, you're almost family. I know we're only distantly related, and that my mother had a distinct nerve dropping me on Ena, when she couldn't be bothered with me herself.'

'Hush now, don't be upsetting yourself. You know full well Ena loved having you.'

'I can't marry Donald. I don't think I'll ever marry. The way my mother lived was enough to put me off marriage for life. She's working on her fifth husband now. The last time I saw her she was wearing all her previous wedding and engagement rings. It was rather horrible, somewhat like an Indian brave wearing his scalps on his belt to show how many men he'd destroyed. I hated that way of life. I know I shouldn't keep coming back here for my holidays. It's not fair to Donald, but this place is the nearest thing to home that I've ever known.'

'Don't sound so forlorn, my pet.' Jeannie put her arm round the younger girl and gave her a hug. 'Of course this is your home, the same as it is mine and it is Donald's. Don't you dare stay away because that foolish lump of a brother has fallen in love with you. He'll get over it just fine.'

'Do you really believe that?' Katriona asked hopefully.

'Of course I believe it,' Jeannie replied briskly. 'Or at least he'll come to terms with it, which is the same thing. He's a born romantic, that brother of mine ... he'll stay a little in love with you always. But he'll settle for that and quite sensibly marry some sweet little lass from the Island. He will be very happy with her and she with him, and they will rear a fine clutch of children. And that's the truth.'

Katriona giggled. 'I'm so relieved. I've been feeling quite

wretched about the whole thing. I know he's going to propose and I've been dreading the day. It seems such a scurvy way to treat you both when you've been so kind to me.'

'Fiddlesticks! You've never been less than honest with Donald, and you can't fall in love to suit your friends. But about yourself, Katriona ...' Jeannie hesitated before going on. 'I never met your mother, but I've heard a great deal about her from you and from Ena. I am of the opinion that she is a very immature person, insecure too, always needing a new man to love her. You must not judge all men by the behaviour of your mother's companions, nor on her experience of marriage. Why, if you feel like that, are you so happy for Bruce and me?'

'But you and Bruce are made for each other,' Katriona protested.

Jeannie laughed gaily. 'That's true. So why not believe that somewhere there is a man who is made only for you?'

'I hope not,' Katriona answered vehemently. 'He'll have a very lonely life if he's waiting for me. It's right for some, but not for me. I despise most men. Not Donald nor Bruce, nor Mr Drummond, but in general they're not up to much. You see, I saw too much of love when I was small. My mother could twist most men around her little finger. She could praise them and flatter them and make them feel like kings, and they would be crazy about her. That would satisfy her for a wee while, then she would treat them like dirt, and they would grovel. It was humiliating, it was degrading ... great big grown men. I couldn't understand it when I was a child and I still can't understand it. Those men, they were much more intelligent than she was, much stronger than she was, some of them very wealthy and holding important public positions, yet she could reduce them to miserable lapdogs.'

'Poor fellows,' Jeannie said softly. 'They must have loved your mother very much, and what an ugly, painful experience it must have been for them. And for you too, Katriona. You say you have seen too much of love when you were small. I do not think you saw much real love at all. Lust, maybe, greed, pride, vanity, you saw, but not genuine honest love. I think you have grown up with a worm's eye view of the world and of people, and I find it sad ...'

Katriona stood up abruptly. 'I don't think it's sad, I think I've been exceedingly fortunate. I don't walk through life waiting for some dimwitted Prince Charming to come and rescue me, the way some stupid girls dream. I go to work happily, and I'm good at my work, because I know that's where my security lies. I don't have to be beholden to my mother for favours. I don't have to wait for her to call me to her side when she's having one of her rare maternal spells, or wait for the odd moment when she's feeling generous to throw some money my way. I can support myself, thank God, and I have no intention of cluttering up my life for any man.'

Jeannie got to her feet slowly, and chuckled, 'Poor wee girlie, you're in for an awful shock one of these days. I can see a man who'll come storming into your life, not noticing all those prickly barriers you've erected. He will only see what he wants to see, not a bitter angry young girl but an honest, very beautiful young woman, who is also highly intelligent and who possesses a warm and loving heart, and a rare generosity.'

'Who are you?' Katriona jeered. 'A seer? You should set up like the gypsies and tell fortunes. Did you get my "man" from the same place as you got Donald's sweet young wife and his brood of children? I hope not, because I almost believed in them. Oh, you're *ridiculous*! I'm off to change for church. Beautiful—huh! What an imagination!'

Katriona raced upstairs, torn between anger and hysterical laughter. Oh, Jeannie was a right comic. She heard Jeannie greet the returning Donald.

'Oh, Katriona. She went upstairs in a fine red-headed rage because I said she was beautiful and had a generous nature.'

Donald sounded puzzled. 'Strange reason for getting into

a temper. Katriona *is* beautiful.'

Katriona lingered by the window long enough to hear Jeannie say with a laugh. 'Just try telling her so, and she'll box your ears! She is convinced that she is still the skinny carrot-topped teenager with the gap-toothed smile and freckles who came here from school for her holidays.'

Well, so she was, or is, thought Katriona as she changed into her elegant Edinburgh suit. She glanced into the mirror and twitched her skirt into place. Fine feathers made fine birds. Actually she resembled a well-dressed broom handle, nothing more. She had no nice womanly curves like Jeannie. She took a closer look at the mirror trying to be objective. Beautiful she wasn't ... that much was certain. But she had changed a little. Maybe her hair could now be described as rich auburn if you had a vivid imagination. She still had that annoying gap between her front teeth, and she still had freckles, just a few. Her face was all angles ... like a badly drawn triangle. She saved her one good feature until the last, her delicately arched eyebrows and very dark, very long eyelashes, which made her blue eyes not so bad. Suddenly impatient, she rammed a smart blue cap on her somewhat subdued red curls, and went downstairs.

Donald joined her a few minutes before Jeannie, and with a wicked grin remarked, 'Very fetching. I would say very beautiful except Jeannie warned me not to. She said you would fetch me a clip on the lug if I paid you a compliment. You would never do that to me, would you, Katriona Carmichael?'

'I would indeed,' Katriona informed him firmly. 'If anyone is beautiful, it's yourself in your Sunday best, Donald. You're a remarkably handsome man.'

'That is the truth,' Donald answered complacently.

'My, my, and you're so modest with it,' Katriona teased.

'It is my worst failing, my modesty,' Donald assured her solemnly.

Jeannie came flying down the stairs. 'Come away, you two, and stop your nonsense. I cannot abide being late for church.'

An hour later when the service was over Katriona walked out into the sunshine, feeling at peace with the world. It was a wonderful old church, and the singing as always had been simply glorious, and the sermon sincere and forthright.

People gathered in small groups, exchanging news and stories of the happenings of the island. Standing with Jeannie and Donald Katriona enjoyed the way they could change from English to the Gaelic without even being aware of it. It did not bother her that she could not follow the conversation all the time. She loved hearing the lilting, laughing language, and watching the animated gesture and expression of the speakers.

Katriona knew the odd word, and heard her own name mentioned several times as Jeannie chatted with a woman who worked at the Lodge.

'Elspeth was after saying that they have a New Zealander staying at the Lodge,' Jeannie translated for Katriona's benefit.

'Interesting,' said Katriona. 'Has he kin on the island? Or does he know someone from here?'

'No, he has no kin on the island. The way Elspeth tells it, he is trying to find a girl by the name of Katriona Carmichael who is holidaying here.'

Katriona's expression changed from mild interest to shock, followed by disbelief, then anger. Her blue eyes flashed. 'Blood and sand! Did he give his name? Oh, please find out, Jeannie!'

'That is an awful expression for a lady to use,' Jeannie gently reproved her.

'I'm sorry. Mr Drummond uses it as an appropriate oath on specially provoking occasions, and I've got a horrid feeling that Elspeth's answer is going to provoke me ... not to mention spoil my holiday.'

Slightly mollified, Jeannie turned and questioned Elspeth, and Katriona listened alertly to the flood of Gaelic she got in reply. She did not need Jeannie to confirm the name; she knew it already.

'His name is Morgan Grant,' Jeannie said at last. 'And I cannot see how he can spoil your holiday. Elspeth says he's a fine young man, with lovely manners. In fact she is quite taken with him. Says he has "the look of an islander", which is high praise indeed. And she is no mean judge of character.'

'I don't care if he comes fur-trimmed and gift-wrapped,' Katriona replied furiously. 'He tried to see me at the office before I came on holiday and I refused to see him. How *dare* he follow me up here?'

Jeannie laughed. 'Obviously a very determined young man. Is he in love with you, Katriona? I am looking forward to meeting him, and that's the truth.'

'Well, I'm not,' Katriona said savagely. 'He's one of the endless supply of idle young men my mother sends on to see me. Honestly, Jeannie, they're *awful*! It eases her conscience to say to any of her set who are travelling to this country, "Do pop in and see my darling wee girl, when you're in Edinburgh. I worry about her so!"' Katriona mocked her mother's syrupy voice, then resumed her natural tone. 'Please, Jeannie, I beg of you, ask Elspeth not to tell him where I'm staying. Stall him off until I leave on the boat in the morning.'

'Don't fret yourself,' Jeannie advised.

'I *am* upset. Why should I have the last day of my holiday ruined by one of Mother's ridiculous young men? Without fail, they've been hard-drinking, racy, money-laden young bores. I've avoided most of them of late, but this fellow is ill-mannered in the extreme, to persist to such lengths.'

Donald, who had joined them and picked up the thread of the discussion, put his arm around her protectively. 'There now, my wee girl, just you leave it all to Jeannie. She will explain it to Elspeth, and we will go to the car. No one will be troubling you while you are staying with us.'

They went out to the car, and were joined a few minutes later by Jeannie, who was having trouble controlling her laughter. 'Elspeth has given me her word not to mention where you are staying. But she says this man has already arranged to hire a car for the day and is taking old Alex as his guide. Elspeth is Alex's cousin. Elspeth says Alex will have a wonderfully happy day visiting from house to house seeing all his old friends, and having a dram here and a dram there. She will tell him not to visit our end of the island so that you will be quite safe at Balephuill.'

Donald chuckled as he drove off. 'I'm feeling it in my heart to be sorry for the rich young man. Alex can be an old devil when he sets out to enjoy himself. I can see him spending a wee while at each house, seemingly enquiring about your whereabouts but being deliberately vague. He will manage to have the time of his life.'

'I'm pleased that Alex will have such a fine time, and I'll enjoy my day all the more each time I think of Morgan Grant becoming more and more tired, impatient and frustrated. It will serve him right following me up here.'

The afternoon flew by on golden wings. After lunch the children from the farm spent a delightful hour with Katriona and Donald down by the shore. They chased the waves along the smooth sandy beach, played in and out the rocks and pools, before wending their way home along the burn, which was bordered with a fantastic display of wild blue iris in bloom. The children sang their way along, their sweet young voices rising clear and true on the fine Highland air.

After returning the children to the house by the loch, Donald and Katriona walked on to Kenavarra. The sun was hot and warm on their backs, and the tiny wildflowers spread a carpet for their feet to walk on.

'Let's sit here for a while,' Donald said as they stood on the grassy slope above the Caves of Kenavarra, watching the sea pounding on the rocks below.

The sky was filled with the angry wheeling gulls calling warning of intruders in their nesting grounds, and the cliffs from top to bottom were a glorious kaleidoscope of pink, green and white: the bright flowers of the sea pinks, the vivid green of the leaves and grasses and the snowy whiteness of the nesting gulls. The crashing of the waves on the sharp rocks below merged with the shrieking of the gulls to make a wild sweet symphony of sound, hauntingly beautiful.

Katriona sat down by Donald, feeling washed in sunlight, music and colour.

After a long companionable silence Donald put his arm around her slim shoulders. 'You love it here, Katriona. I love you being here. Why not say you'll marry me and spend the rest of your life on Tiree?'

When Katriona did not answer he continued, 'We would be very happy, I can promise you that. You are not a city girl. You always say that the children here have a wonderful life ... well, your children and mine would grow up in the same way. Say yes, my darling wee Katriona, please say yes.'

Katriona did not pull away from his caress, in fact she leaned closer towards him, her cheek resting against the roughness of his tweed jacket. 'Oh, Donald, what can I say? You're my friend. More than that, you're my family, almost. I *do* love you, but ... but not in the marrying way. In fact I doubt I'm the marrying kind of girl. Please, don't take it badly. I can't bear to think I would hurt you, when you've always been so very kind to me.'

'You could not hurt me if you tried.' Donald brushed her bright hair with his lips.

Katriona thought she would choke on the hard lump in her throat, yet she had to explain her answer to him a little more. She owed him that much. 'Thank you, Donald. You see, I don't know how much I'm like my mother ... perhaps more than I care to think. I've seen her marry three times, and each time she's convinced it's the only time she's ever loved, and that it will last a lifetime, then after a year or two it all comes apart. How do I know that I haven't inherited her nature, that I wouldn't be as fickle and inconsistent as her, that I wouldn't end up hurting anyone who loved me, that I wouldn't be careless with my children? I wouldn't want to take that chance. I've thought it all through and marriage is not for me. Please accept that as the truth.'

Donald hugged her close for a moment, then got to his feet and held his hands out to her, pulling her to her feet and into his arms. 'Your pretty blue eyes are filled with tears, my wee girl. You must not cry for me, darling. You haven't hurt me ... I am disappointed, naturally, but I felt all along that your answer would be no. But we can still be friends. As for that rubbish about taking after your mother, forget it all. Your mother is a vain, shallow, spoiled woman, and you do not favour her in any way. As you grow older you will get more confidence in yourself, and I have no doubt that when you love a man enough to marry him you will remain through the years a loyal and loving wife and a fine example to your children.'

Katriona abandoned any attempt to hold back her tears. It was just so like Donald to be thinking of her and trying to comfort her, instead of feeling put down and sorry for himself. 'Oh, Donald I do *love* you! I feel so wretched.'

'But not wretched enough to marry me?' His smile was a little askew. 'Not to worry, I'll settle for next best place, that of a loved and trusted friend. Now we must away home to Jeannie or she will be thinking we've fallen over the cliffs.'

Catching hold of her hand, he raced her crazily down the hill so they arrived breathless and laughing at the track which led homeward across the *marrah*, the common land shared by the crofters.

When they arrived back at the croft there was a note on the table saying Jeannie had gone across to Balemartin to visit with friends, and would Donald please collect her.

'Will you drive with me, Katriona?' Donald asked as he prepared to take the car out.

'No. If you don't mind I'll stay here for a spell, but I'll open the yard gate for you.'

She ran lightly ahead of him and swung the gate wide, then waved as he drove through. He would only be away about half an hour, so she fastened the gate and climbed up on it to wait for their return.

Suddenly her interest was caught by a figure of a man

striding across the front pasture from the direction of the
neighbours' house. Katriona idly tried to guess his identity.
She knew most of the local people, but she did not recognise
him. As he drew closer she could see he was dark and very
tall, a lean but broad-built fellow. He was coming at a
terrific pace. He would be upset to find Donald not at home.
She was almost tempted to call out to him to save his energy.

It was not until he cleared the last fence impatiently and
was striding towards her that a horrible premonition hit
her. It struck her like an electric shock, making her para-
lysed for an instant, her fingers and toes tingling with pins
and needles of fear. She swung her leg over the other side
of the gate in preparation for leaping down and running
for the croft, when her arm was caught in a grip of iron.

'Oh, no you don't, my girl. You *are* Katriona Carmichael, don't bother denying it!'

'Why should I deny it? Let me go!' Katriona shouted.
'Take your hands off me!' She glared up at the man now
astride the gate. He was not only angry, he was boiling mad.

'Let you go? You must be joking. What a good laugh you
must have had knowing I was being given a fine old run-
around by your friend Alex. The artful old dodger had me
completely foxed most of the day. What a dance he's led
me!' He gave Katriona a vigorous shake as he landed on
the ground beside her. 'Well, what have you got to say for
yourself?'

Katriona laughed up into his face, taunting him. 'I'm
delighted you had such a bad day.' She twisted her wrist
trying to make him release the grip of his strong brown
hand. 'Let me go!'

'Not likely. You knew I had to speak to you. I told you,
when I was speaking to you on the phone in Edinburgh, that
it was important. You could have given me five minutes of
your precious time instead of haring away up here to this
godforsaken island where most of the inhabitants can't
speak English.'

Katriona laughed nastily. 'Huh! That was only for your
benefit. They're friends of mine. They can all speak and

understand English perfectly well. In fact they speak it beautifully, far better than a Colonial like you.'

'I suspected as much.' The flashing grey eyes lost none of their fury. 'Well, you can stand shouting here at me till the cows come home for all I care. Or you can get a little sense and take me back up to the house, where I'll speak my piece. Then I'll be only too happy to let you go your way and I'll go mine.'

'I have nothing to say to you,' Katriona spat the words out. 'How did you find me?'

'I purchased a map of the island before I came, and marked the roads Alex took me, and each time I suggested this area he came all over coy and pretended he had definite ... or almost definite ... news of your visiting a home in the opposite direction. As the afternoon wore on and he partook more and more freely of the grand hospitality which we were offered, he became a trifle careless. If you want to see him he's over next door, feeling considerably chastened at his failure to complete the job.' Morgan Grant jerked her arm. 'Now come along up to the house.'

'It's not your house!' Katriona's eyes flashed.

'No, it's not my house. And it's not your house ... yet. But we're going to use it. *Move!*'

'No!' Katriona planted her two feet firmly apart and scowled ferociously up at her captor. 'You may be able to intimidate an old man, but you can't frighten me.'

'I wouldn't count on it. My name is Morgan Grant. I've had a very long and tiring day. I'm very nearly at the end of my patience. I've wasted more than enough time on you already, but come hell or high water I will deliver a message I brought from Ian Carmichael, and I will do it in a civilised fashion up there in that house. Now, you may not know me very well, but folks back home could tell you I'm not a man to be scared by an ill-tempered, ill-mannered, pint-sized redhead. So either get walking or on the count of three I'll pick you up and sling you over my shoulder, and ... One ... two ...'

Katriona started for the croft, her soft young mouth set

in a grim straight line. She would not admit she was scared, but the way his voice had got quieter and quieter as he was speaking made her more nervous than if he had yelled at her. She opened the door and said through gritted teeth, 'Do come in.'

'Thank you very much.' Morgan Grant released her wrist and walked over and sat down in Donald's comfortable chair by the fireplace. 'Sit down, this won't take long.'

'I prefer to stand,' Katriona returned icily. His confidence and easy air of assurance as he walked in and took over Donald's house and Donald's chair infuriated her.

'*Sit down!*' Morgan Grant thundered, and made to rise from his chair.

Katriona hastily chose a nearby chair. 'Don't get too comfortable. Donald will be back soon and he'll throw you off his land when I tell him how outrageously you've behaved towards me.'

Morgan Grant laughed sarcastically. 'Oh, yes, he's the poor chap who wants to marry you—I picked up an endless amount of useless information as I visited around today. Do I offer him my congratulations or my condolences when we meet?'

Katriona wanted to scream and hit out at him, even throw Jeannie's favourite vase at him. She could not ever remember being so angry or so humiliated. 'And Elspeth said you had *lovely* manners!'

His eyes narrowed. 'And when was this?'

'At church this morning,' Katriona stammered, realising that in her temper she had given away more than she meant to.

His grey eyes flashed fire and Katriona's heart skipped a nervous beat. 'So you did know I was here. I'd given old Alex the benefit of the doubt. Well, we'll soon clear up our business, and I can go back to ...'

'Our business?' Katriona interrupted sharply. 'I have no business to share with you. And before you start, allow me to inform you that I'm not interested in any message that you may have to deliver to me from my mother.'

'I haven't come from your mother,' Grant told her bluntly. 'Now if you'd keep quiet for a few minutes ... No, better still, if you'd answer a few direct questions clearly and precisely, I'll be on my way within five minutes. First, do you recognise the name Ross Carmichael?'

'No.'

'Think carefully. Have you ever heard it mentioned, say, when you were a child?'

'No.' Katriona snapped out the answer each time.

Morgan Grant drew a deep breath as if barely able to control his temper. 'Then perhaps we can attack this problem from a different angle.'

'I haven't got a problem,' Katriona informed him with a toss of her red curls. 'You have a problem.'

He ignored her interjection. 'Could you please tell me the name of your father?'

Katriona gasped, the colour rushed to her cheeks, then receded, leaving her face starkly pale. Her eyes, huge and darkly blue with shock, stared back at him for an instant, then her long lashes fanned her cheeks and her reaction was hidden from him.

She slipped her hands into her jacket pocket so that he could not see them shaking and clenched them so tightly shut that she could feel her nails biting into the soft flesh of her palms.

'Oh, come on now, let's get this over and done with,' Morgan Grant persisted. If her eyes had been open she would have seen the puzzled expression on his face, but she did not even notice the softer tone in his voice.

Nothing registered with Katriona, nothing except her own pain and shock. All her life she had been expecting this question. All her life she had been terrified of being asked that straightforward question. She had often had sickening nightmares when she was younger, about this very situation ... someone shouting and demanding her father's name, not giving her time to be evasive, yelling at her so that she came right out with the ugly truth: that she was illegitimate. Strange that it had never happened before.

Usually people asked casually, and she was well practised in answering in an equally casual manner. She had a whole string of answers, such as ... he left my mother when I was tiny ... or, my mother divorced him when I was a baby ... but they only worked because of the careless way she spoke them. This time it was different.

She took a deep breath and opened her eyes and spoke fiercely. 'I don't know who you are, Morgan Grant, nor do I know what authority you think you have to be able to come here and question me about my family. It doesn't matter if you have authority or not, because I refuse to answer any of your questions. I think you're arrogant, ignorant, and a nosey-parker. So you may now leave. There's nothing to hinder you. The door is open.'

'I'm not leaving until I do have some answers,' Morgan Grant said quietly. 'I'm not prying into your private life for a mere whim. My boss, Ross Carmichael of Evangeline ... that's a sheep station in the South Island of New Zealand ... asked me to come here and check you out.'

'Well, you've checked,' Katriona cried vehemently, 'and I'm not the girl you're looking for. I don't know Ross Carmichael. I've never heard of him, and believe me, I never want to hear of him or you in the future.' She stood up. 'If you won't leave then I will.' She walked to the far door.

'Just a minute!' Morgan Grant spoke sharply. 'If you've never heard of him, why are you claiming that he's your father?'

Katriona whirled around. 'That's a downright lie!'

'My opinion exactly,' Morgan Grant said smoothly. 'Still, my boss was insistent that I meet you and talk with you and form an objective opinion on the case. Believe me, I find this mission as distasteful as you apparently do. I thought all along that the letter was a hoax. So if you'd only calm down and answer one question, or let me explain ...'

'No!'

'Oh, do be reasonable.' He sounded more exasperated than angry.

'I *am* being reasonable. I have no intention of listening

to any more of your gobbledegook. You're "away with the fairies", and that's my own not entirely objective opinion.' Katriona's voice was scathing. 'The car has just stopped and in a few moments you can explain your position to Donald and Jeannie, and how you came to be alone and un-invited in their home.'

He gave a short laugh. 'Donald being the one who's going to throw me off his land. I hope he's big enough for the job.'

Katriona slammed the door behind her and took the stairs to her room two at a time. She had no doubt that Donald would handle the situation efficiently without re-sorting to brute strength. Well ... she hoped he would, because that man from New Zealand was taller than Don-ald, broader than Donald, and much much meaner and nastier than Donald could ever be. He could only be described as a formidable proposition.

She hurried to the window which overlooked the yard, expecting at any moment to see Donald ushering Morgan Grant out of the gate. The minutes passed slowly as she waited and she became more and more impatient. At last she could stand it no longer, and opened her door and stood at the top of the stairs, trying to catch the drift of the conversation. There was no angry upraised voice, just the pleasant rise and fall of conversation between people enjoying a talk. Then she heard them laughing.

It was too much! She stalked back into her room and closed the door firmly. She would have liked to bang it shut. She should have known that Donald and Jeannie would find it impossible to be rude to a stranger under their roof. Katriona began to throw her clothes into her suitcase. She would not go downstairs while Morgan Grant was there.

At last she heard the car drive off and Jeannie calling up the stairs. 'Katriona, come down. Supper is ready, and Morgan could not stay. Donald has driven him back to Alex and the car.'

Blast Donald! Blast Highland hospitality! And most of

all blast that dratted Morgan Grant. He had spoiled her holiday. She had *known* he would. She should have stayed downstairs and denounced him. Instead she had left him in control of the situation while she was trapped sulking in her bedroom. He had put her in the wrong and she hated him for it.

She joined Jeannie by the brightly burning open fire. 'Oh, thanks for lighting the fire, Jeannie. It isn't really cold enough for a fire in the evenings, but there's nothing as homely and welcoming as an open fire.'

'I knew you would enjoy it. And it is your last night.' Jeannie smiled sweetly. 'What a nice man that Morgan Grant is—so handsome, and such elegant manners. He said he was truly sorry that he had upset you, and asked me to offer his apologies. We both found him quite charming.'

'*Charming indeed*,' Katriona repeated with a very different inflection in her voice. 'How did he say he'd upset me? And what explanation did he give you for hounding me down like a criminal?'

'Oh, it wasn't like that at all, Katriona,' Jeannie protested with a reproachful glance. 'He said you would not hear him out. He said he was leaving for New Zealand this week, and had only followed you up here because your office would not tell him when you were expected back. You can understand how he would be worried. How could he return to those good people in New Zealand and say that he had failed to contact you? It must have been very difficult for him.'

'My heart bleeds for him,' Katriona remarked sarcastically.

'Here's Donald,' Jeannie said thankfully. 'You two will be looking forward to your meal. Donald said you've been on the go all day.'

Donald joined them at the table. 'Fine fellow that Morgan Grant, Katriona. A pity you two got off to such a bad start. Did Jeannie say he offered his apologies?'

'She did.' Katriona's eyes were smouldering. Oh, Morgan Grant had played a fine confidence trick on these two friends of hers. They would never believe her now if she told them that he had manhandled her, bullied her, and shouted at her. 'So you liked him?'

'Yes, I did. An intelligent and interesting man. He's a farmer, did you know that?'

'No. That didn't come up in our conversation.'

'Oh, yes.' Donald sounded delighted with himself. 'He's very interested in our way of farming here, and was very pleased when I suggested he come back and spend the day with us tomorrow. He said now that he'd spoken with you there was no need to rush away.'

'Did you tell him that I was leaving on the boat early tomorrow morning?' Katriona asked with deceptive sweetness.

'Well now, I don't think I did.' Donald looked surprised. 'You see, we were talking about farming methods most of the time.'

Katriona hooted with laughter, her good humour miraculously restored. Fancy Morgan Grant thinking he had wormed his way into Donald and Jeannie's good grace with a pretended interest in farming, and thinking he had cornered her in her friends' home. Oh, it was delicious! He would come over tomorrow refreshed and ready for battle and she would be well away to sea, having sailed at dawn.

'Did he say to you why he was so anxious to see me?' she asked.

Jeannie smiled with relief at Katriona's change of mood. 'No. He said it was a personal matter. Some people who lived in the same district as he does, and who wanted to contact your mother but had lost her address but vaguely knew where you were ... I may not have it right.'

'I can understand if you're a little confused. I was myself.' Katriona's grin was wide. She wanted to warn these two not to be taken in by that plausible rogue even if he was good-looking and appeared courteous. She wanted to shout at them that he was lying and that his story was a hoax, but she decided to drop the subject of Morgan Grant and enjoy her evening. Oh, he was a cunning man, but she had outwitted him.

Even so, she did not completely relax until next morning when Donald and Jeannie drove down to the wharf at Scarnish and put her on board. Usually when she left the island she would feel sad, but all she could think of was getting away from that wretched man, and the thought of the disappointment in store for him when he arrived at the farm to find her gone made her chuckle wickedly. She walked the deck enjoying the crystal clear morning and the sparkling smooth sea. She always loved this sea trip even if it took five hours, much preferring it to a quick flight in a plane. Whether the sea was rough or smooth, it made no difference because she was an excellent sailor.

After she arrived in Oban there was still the long train trip to Glasgow. Her mind kept going back to the meeting with Morgan Grant. Why had he said she was claiming to be the daughter of Ross Carmichael? And he had mentioned a letter. If he had been a different sort of a man she could have talked with him and sorted it all out. Perhaps she had been a bit hasty. It would have been interesting to find out more. Could her mother have been married to Ross Carmichael? No, that was not possible. Or was it? But if her mother had been married to this Carmichael fellow, then she, Katriona, could be their legitimate daughter. She could have a real father ... a legal father. Oh, it was all rubbish. Her mother would have told her.

Katriona sighed deeply as she gazed out the window of the train at the sunlight glistening on Loch Lomond. Could her mother have kept a secret like that all these years? But why keep it a secret? Her mother had never spoken to Katriona about her father. Many times Katriona had tried to find out something about him, but her mother had always said she was lucky she had never met him, implying that he was a bad lot. Further questioning had only made her angry, and Katriona had learned never to mention the subject as it would put her mother in an evil mood for days.

So she had assumed that she was illegitimate because her mother's maiden name was Carmichael ... but say her mother had been married to a man whose name was the same as hers? Oh, that was ridiculous. But it could happen. Angrily Katriona tried to put further speculation from her mind. But the question crept back again and again. If her mother had been married to Ross Carmichael why keep it a secret? Her mother had never worried about mentioning her other husbands and her other marriages. But then Katriona was old enough to know what was going on.

And that Morgan Grant had not said anything about a marriage. Just that she was claiming to be the daughter of his boss. It was just a mix-up. They had made a mistake because of the name Carmichael. She had never written a letter.

Forget it, Forget it, Forget it, the words clicked through her mind in rhythm with the train's wheels. Tomorrow she would be back at work, and it would be good to be busy, too busy to waste time thinking about that preposterous creature Morgan Grant. She gave an involuntary giggle as she thought of his chagrin on finding her gone from the island. She would never see him again.

The staff greeted her warmly when she arrived at the office next morning and by lunch time she was so much involved she felt that she had never been away. There was that disturbing rumour that big changes were afoot. Katriona did not want any big changes in her life, she enjoyed her work and got on fine with Mr Drummond.

Miss Jamieson, the senior buyer for the firm, quelled the younger girl's enthusiasm. 'It's merely a rumour, Katriona, take no notice. Although I must admit that I've heard several snippets that do lend themselves to the merger theory.'

'It must have developed very quickly,' Katriona commented. 'I heard not a whisper about it before I left.'

'Exactly what I was telling the girls. If Miss Carmichael hasn't been informed, then there's no truth in it. We all know what confidence Mr Drummond places in you.'

The intercom crackled and Katriona jumped up. 'Mr Drummond must be back in his office. I haven't seen him yet.'

'Ah, Katriona, nice to have you back. Did you enjoy your holiday? I can see you did. I have missed you. No one could find a thing for me during your absence.'

Katriona smiled warmly at him and said quite truthfully, 'It's a pleasure to be back. And yes, I did have a lovely break. Now, what particular file were you wanting?'

'That thing about Canada. You know, they were sending a rep over here. I've forgotten his name.'

Katriona went swiftly to the filing cabinet and sorted out the required file. It was no wonder that the staff found it hard to trace things when she was away. Mr Drummond could never remember names and relied on Katriona to be his memory bank. It would be impossible to find the file on a man whose name could not be remembered, nor yet the name of a firm he worked for.

'Ah, Katriona, you're more than a secretary,' Mr Drummond said thankfully. 'We'll have to give you a new title, what do you say? Super-secretary or senior office executive, do you favour that?'

'No, thanks. I'm perfectly satisfied with my title,' Katriona replied just as the door burst open and a short, self-important-looking man strode in.

'See here, Drummond, you tell that stupid girl out the front that I don't need escorting to your office each time I visit, nor do I need to be announced each time. I can't seem to get it through her thick head.'

Katriona was shocked by the stranger's behaviour and could see Shona through the open doorway, crimson with humiliation.

'Ah, come in, Prendergast,' Mr Drummond said in an over-hearty voice. He appeared to hesitate for a moment, then his kindly face took on a determined look. He stepped round his desk to confront the visitor. 'I know we have to work together very closely for the next few months, Prendergast, and I would hope we can achieve a good relationship with each other. However, I can't have you upsetting my staff, so I would be grateful if you would apologise to Shona, who was only doing her work as she's been trained to do it. She will continue to announce you each time you arrive, until you take over this office and institute your own staff training methods.'

Katriona felt like applauding. She knew what an effort it must have been for Mr Drummond to insist on an apology for wee Shona, but he had always treated his staff with courtesy and consideration, so it would really go against the grain to see someone walk roughshod over them. The two men eyed each other for several seconds before the visitor wheeled around and went to the door.

'I'll be through in my office if you want me, Mr Drummond,' Katriona spoke softly, giving him an encouraging smile as she went through the communicating door.

He just nodded, still looking troubled by the unpleasantness. She was hardly seated when he summoned her back to his office.

'Ah, Prendergast, I would like you to meet my personal secretary, Miss Carmichael. She's been on holiday these past two weeks. You'll find us a more efficient office now that we're back to full strength.'

'That wouldn't be hard to achieve!' Mr Prendergast gave an unpleasant laugh.

Katriona saw the look of distaste on Mr Drummond's face for an instant before he continued with the introduction. 'And, Katriona my dear, this is Mr Prendergast from Apex Incorporated. Our shareholders wish to expand and have decided to move in with Apex, and Mr Prendergast is the London representative. I'm asking you to give him all the help you can, and he's to have free access to all our papers and books. I'll be retiring very soon. I know this will come as a surprise to you ... it did to me. It's a comfort to me to know you'll be beside me over these next few months, which could be quite strenuous and taxing, and I know Mr Prendergast will appreciate your helpful co-operation.'

Mr Prendergast barely acknowledged the introduction,

and for the rest of the week made Katriona's life and the life of the rest of the staff quite chaotic. Day by day she became more positive that she could not stay on and work for him. If it were not for the real affection she had for Mr Drummond she would have put her notice in immediately. She had to admit that the London man knew his work, that he was energetic, efficient, enthusiastic, and that it was awful working for him. She knew the rest of the staff felt the same way and that they were all looking around for new jobs, but out of a sense of loyalty to Mr Drummond would stay with the firm until he retired.

As the week wore on Katriona was annoyed to find that even with the turmoil in the office she was far from forgetting her meeting with Morgan Grant. She knew it was a waste of time thinking about him, but she could not help herself going back to it again and again. She thought he might have tried to see her again when he left the island. By Friday she was dismayed to find that she was really disappointed that he had not tried to contact her. How could she be so stupid? She *must* put him out of her mind, because he had told Donald he was flying home this week, so of course he had gone.

About four o'clock on Friday afternoon Katriona was rushing through a letter to catch the late mail when Morag, one of the other typists, came in.

'You're pounding that typewriter so hard you didn't hear me knock. Shona is out, so I had to do the reception desk, and there's a gorgeous guy out there asking for you.'

For one second Katriona held her breath, thinking it might be Morgan Grant, then realised how foolish she was. He would be back in New Zealand by now. 'Did you ask what he wanted to see me about? I'm very busy. Is it important? Try Miss Jamieson, see if she can spare the time to see him.'

Morag pulled a long face. 'Really, Katriona, I fear for you. After a week like you've had with that shark from London I think you should leap at the chance to interview this fantastic fellow. He's a Canadian, I think, by his accent ...'

'Drat it! He *is* a Canadian. And I've got to see him. I've been handling all that correspondence for Mr Drummond.'

'You won't be sorry,' Morag remarked with a wink. 'When he said "I want Miss Carmichael" I went all over goosebumps. I'd give my right arm to have him say "I want Miss Watson" in that sexy voice.'

Katriona laughed. 'I do hope he never says it. I'm sure he's not worth such a sacrifice. What babies you all are, Morag, seeing romance in every man. He's not supposed to arrive until next week. Tell Miss Jamieson I may pass him on to her if he looks like lingering. I simply must get these letters away.'

'Why not pass him on to me?' Morag pouted. 'Miss Jamieson wouldn't know what to do with that much man even if she took lessons.'

'Out!' cried Katriona with a wave of her hand. With fingers flying she managed to complete the letter before she heard Morag knock on the door. She ripped the letter from the typewriter as she called 'Come in' without looking up. 'Morag, could you take this through for Mr Drummond before you go. If he wants any alterations done bring it back, otherwise post it when he's signed it.'

Morag took the letter as Katriona swung around to face her visitor. 'Good afternoon, Mr ...'

'Grant is the name, Morgan Grant. I would like to thank you for sparing me a few minutes of your valuable time, Miss Carmichael. I understand you're very busy, so I won't keep you.'

Katriona froze, unable to speak.

Morgan Grant appeared to be relaxed and completely at ease. 'I would like to apologise for my behaviour at our first meeting. I had no right to come storming into your life the way I did. I'm leaving on the plane tonight and came to ask you if you could meet me for dinner after you finish work. We could then discuss the situation like two reasonable adults. Well, what do you say?'

Katriona with a tremendous effort managed to collect her thoughts. The expression 'storming into your life' felt very familiar and she was trying to remember where she had heard it recently. Suddenly it came back, and colour flooded her face as she remembered Jeannie saying about a man coming storming into her life. 'Thank you for your apology, Mr Grant, but I don't see what useful purpose can be served . . .' She got to her feet.

The tall dark tanned man smiled at her. 'Really, Miss Carmichael, if you're at all honest, you must admit to a tiny bit of curiosity.'

'Curiosity killed the cat,' Katriona replied smartly. No wonder Jeannie and Elspeth found him charming! And Morag was quite correct, Miss Jamieson would need lessons to cope with Morgan Grant. But Katriona wasn't fooled by his change of front. He might be able to steal a woman's heart away with his smile, but underneath that surface charm he was a nasty arrogant bully . . .

'I'm sure nothing so drastic will happen to you.' He laughed down at her, his grey eyes warm and friendly. 'What time do you finish here?'

'About six, but . . .'

'Splendid. I'll be waiting for you.'

Before Katriona could protest he strode from the room. She sat down, her heart beating wildly. She felt as if a tornado had swept through the office. She thought of all the beautifully sarcastic answers she could have come up with, had he given her time. It was maddening to think that she had let him take complete control of the conversation. But she *did* want to know why he came to see her, and where the letter came into it, and who wrote it. Oh, he was so wrong, she was not only a tiny bit curious . . . she was eaten up with curiosity.

'Mr Drummond said for you to change this figure, Katriona, then post it off. He said sorry that he gave you the wrong amount.' Morag dropped the letter back on the desk. 'Hey! He's gone. Wasn't he fantastic?'

'I presume you mean Mr Grant? Yes, he's gone.'

'You're not at all excited about having a man like that calling on you? You must be made of ice. Talk about *impact*! Honestly, if I'd been you I wouldn't have let him out of the office until I'd kidded him into making a date ... even if it meant blackmailing him. You'll never get another chance like that.'

'I think Miss Jamieson will make an impact on you too, Morag, if you don't get back to your work.' Katriona started to sort through some papers on her desk. She really must concentrate on finishing these quotations today. That Morgan Grant was having the most peculiar effect on her. She had almost boasted to Morag that she did have a date with him tonight, if only to prove that she was human after all.

At ten to six she covered her typewriter and went through to the cloakroom to freshen up. After she had made some hasty repairs to her make-up and added a touch of perfume, she gazed at her reflection in the mirror with utter dissatisfaction. She wished she had time to go home and change. Her suit was neat and functional ... an office suit, nothing more, nothing less ... If only she had time to get her hair trimmed ...

Shocked, she realised that she was wanting to make a good impression on Morgan Grant. How *ridiculous*! After tonight she would never see him again. What did it matter how she looked?

She marched out through the office building switching the lights off as she went, checking to see if all the windows were shut. She carefully locked the outside door behind her and dropped the keys in her bag before turning to face Morgan Grant.

'Good evening, Katriona.' He seemed amused about something. 'I have a taxi waiting. I've ordered dinner early at my hotel. I think you'll enjoy the meal, they have an excellent chef.'

'Good evening,' Katriona replied, annoyed to hear her voice wobble nervously. She wasn't frightened of him, it was just that she had trouble breathing when she got too

close to him. And it was a bit difficult to know how to behave when they had been shouting insults at each other the
last time they were together on the Island.

She sat silent during their taxi ride and then followed
him meekly into the very elegant hotel. Seated primly at the
table she studied the menu as if it was a matter of life
and death what she chose to eat. Then she become aware
that the large menu was shaking badly as her hands
trembled and she knew it was a dead giveaway. She put it
down stiffly and told him she was happy to have whatever
he ordered.

Throughout the well-chosen, beautifully cooked and pre-
sented meal, she hardly spoke one word. She couldn't. It
was all she could do to give an appearance of normality by
concentrating fully on the food and wine. Once, only once
she had looked directly at Morgan Grant in answer to a
question and found him watching her with such intensity
that it left her breathless. She had not repeated that error.
She knew he was completely relaxed and enjoying himself,
and that burned her up.

No man should be as handsome as he was. She could
hear the laughter in his voice as he spoke of his trip to the
Island. He did not seem to notice that she only answered in
monosyllables, or if he did notice he did not care. He
talked of everything under the sun except the things she
wanted to know. She wanted to hear about New Zealand
... about the man Ross Carmichael. She tried to tell herself
that she was unused to dining out in fashionable hotels, but
knew it wasn't true. She had always been in and out of these
places with her mother. She told herself she wasn't used to
dining out with men. That was true enough. But she had
dined out with young men often enough to know that she
was usually bored to the back teeth by their company.

Tonight she was far from bored. She risked another
glance across the table and wished she had not. Morgan
Grant had impact, and he knew it.

He told the waiter that they would have their coffee in
the lounge, and guided Katriona across the dining room

and over to two comfortable chairs and an occasional table in a secluded corner.

When he offered her a cigarette she refused, and he put the packet back in his pocket and settled back comfortably in his chair.

'I don't mind if you want to smoke,' Katriona said politely.

'Thank you, but I won't. It's a bad habit. I'm trying to give it up.'

'Are you succeeding?' she asked.

'Yes. I don't often fail when I put my mind to something.' His smile was wicked.

Katriona was furious at herself for giving him that opening. He was so smug and sure of himself, it just made her feel more inadequate than ever.

'Do you know anyone by the name of Ena McIlroy?'

'Ena McIlroy!' Katriona jerked forward in her chair in surprise at the question. 'Ena McIlroy was a distant relation of my mother's. She died almost two years ago.'

'Would you say she was an honest responsible person?' Morgan asked.

'None more honest than Ena,' Katriona said forthrightly. She was aware now that there was no amusement in his intelligent grey eyes. It was replaced by an alert, wary expression.

'Strange you should say that ... everyone else is of the same opinion.'

'It would be strange if they were not,' Katriona stated fiercely. 'She was a fine person. Dearly loved and highly respected.'

'The letter my boss received was written by her. She claims that you're Ross Carmichael's daughter.'

CHAPTER TWO

KATRIONA gasped. It was so completely unexpected. Her blue eyes opened wide with shock. 'Ena wrote to this Carmichael man claiming I was his daughter!'

'Correct.'

'But ... but why should she do that? She never mentioned anything like that to me.' Katriona still sounded incredulous. She sat silent for a moment or two. 'So he heard nearly two years ago that I might be his daughter. He must have been crazy with delight the way he rushed to verify the news.'

'You do him an injustice,' Morgan straightened up in his chair. 'He received the letter last month. Ena McIlroy had left it with her lawyer to post when you reached the age of twenty-one. She'd apparently promised your mother she wouldn't tell you the truth about your father. When she knew she was dying she tried to persuade your mother to tell you and your mother told her she would ... when you were twenty-one. Ena McIlroy must have known your mother very well, because she didn't trust her to keep her word. The lawyer said the old lady felt very strongly that the secret must not die with her, so she told him to post the letter to Ross Carmichael a week after your birthday. That's why the lawyer held it so long.'

Katriona stared at him in bewilderment. If Ena said Ross Carmichael was her father, she wanted no further proof. Ena would never tell a lie. Her mind whirled with questions. Why was it a secret? Was her mother married to the man or not? Was that why it was a secret? If she was married to him then she, Katriona, had a real father.

'I'm afraid this must have come as a bit of a shock to you.' Morgan sounded really concerned. 'Would you like a brandy?'

40

Katriona shook her head.

'Well, here's the coffee. Drink it up while it's hot. I'm sorry it never occurred to me that you wouldn't be in on it.'

Katriona reached for the cup and drank the hot coffee with gratitude ... it seemed to settle her nerves. Then she realised what Morgan had said to her, and her blue eyes flashed with anger. 'So that's it! It was your attitude which bothered me. You thought it was a hoax ... the letter, I mean. You thought it was some scheme thought up by Ena and myself. How *dare* you think that? And you have a colossal nerve coming here checking up on her character and mine. Well, my man, you can go right back to New Zealand and tell Ross Carmichael and anyone else who's remotely interested in your investigations to stop worrying. I don't care if he's my father or not. Why should I need another father? I've had my choice of fathers ... four to be exact, and another one coming up. What I don't need most is another father!'

'Calm down,' Morgan said soothingly. 'Naturally I had to check her out, and I'm sorry if I gained the wrong impression from the letter. Ross Carmichael is not a poor man.'

'*Charming!*' Katriona was scathing. 'So his first thought on hearing he has a daughter is to protect his assets. She would naturally only be interested in his money. What else? As if I'd want to be related to a man like that!'

'Cut that out!' Morgan spoke sharply. 'You're deliberately putting the wrong interpretation on everything I say. Why don't you stop and listen before you hit the panic button? The boss asked me to come over here and see if there was any truth in the story ...'

'Huh!' Katriona interrupted sarcastically. 'He doesn't even know if he was married to my mother. That makes us even, I don't know either. He doesn't even know if he's met her or slept with her or if she had a child by him. He sounds a pretty poor specimen to me. And if anyone's story is thin it's yours.'

'Of course he knows he was married to Fiona Carmichael. It was the biggest mistake of his life. He was married to her for two years ... well, she lived with him for two years. Then he had a severe accident and the doctors didn't think he would ever walk again. While he was lying critically ill in hospital your mother cleared out and left him. What do you think that did to him? Now, some twenty years later, he hears from someone he doesn't know that she had a child six months after she arrived in Scotland and stating that he's supposed to be the father. Is it any wonder that he thought it was a scheme set up by you and your mother to get money out of him?'

Katriona turned pale, her hands gripped the arms of the chair until her knuckles turned white. How could she defend her mother from such accusations? Worse still, knowing her mother's character, the story was probably true. Well, she had found out all she wanted to know. In her own mind she knew that she had found her father. She knew who had written the letter ... her own darling Ena McIlroy.

Shading her face with her hand, she avoided Morgan's searching eyes. Dear Ena, darling Ena. It almost seemed as if she had reached back from the grave to reassure Katriona that she was loved. Ena had been the only stable influence in Katriona's crazy mixed up life, the only person she could count on to remain exactly the same even though she was parted from her years at a time.

'Say, are you okay?' Morgan leaned across and touched Katriona's shoulder.

She looked across at him, her eyes bright with unshed tears, and her face had a soft vulnerable expression. 'I'm sorry. It's just a bit much to take in all at once. You see, Ena knew ... she was the only one who knew I was ... a bit hung-up about having no father. It must have been so very difficult for her, wanting to tell me, yet held by the promise she'd given my mother. She used to tell me so often that it didn't matter who my parents were, that what I made myself in this world was the important thing, that we're each responsible for our own actions.'

Katriona was not aware that the tears were sliding down her cheeks, that she looked young and totally defenceless. She only knew that the hurt and humiliation of past years were suddenly wiped away and that Ena had done this for her. 'I know also there are hundreds of children who never know who their parents are, or never know and meet their father, and who aren't bothered about it at all. But it bothered me, and that's the truth.' Her voice was husky with emotion. 'It seems that Ena has given me one more wonderful gift to add to all those she gave me through the years.'

'I'm glad to be the person who brought you some good news,' Morgan said gently. 'You have no doubt but that she wrote the truth?'

The glowing look left Katriona's face and she was instantly on the defensive again, hastily brushing the tears away. 'I believe it, and I don't care much whether you believe it or not.'

Morgan laughed, 'I've gathered that my opinions are not important to you. Still, I have yet to complete the job I came to do.' He reached into the pocket of his well-cut suit and took out his wallet. 'When I left New Zealand Ross said to contact you, and if I decided that you were the genuine article I was to give you this bank draft. It should cover your return air fare from here to Christchurch and a bit over for expenses.'

He put an envelope on the occasional table.

Katriona glared at him. 'Genuine article—what a way to describe me! And what happened if I was a phoney? Or if you weren't too sure either way?'

'Simple, quite simple. If you were a phoney, I was to sort you out. If I had any reasonable doubt I was to give you the draft anyway and Ross would make the final decision when you got out there.'

'You sort me out. Huh!' Katriona snorted. 'You and who else? Fancy sending a boy on a man's job! And what makes him so sure that I'd want to go rushing out to New Zealand? As a matter of fact I have no intention whatsoever of going, so you can take his petty cash back to him with my compliments.' She flipped the envelope towards Morgan.

'Oh, don't be so childish and ridiculous. Take it. You just went all dewy-eyed about finding you had a legal father. Don't try and convince me you're not wanting to meet him.'

'I don't want to meet him,' Katriona cried fiercely. 'I prefer not to. I only wanted to know that he really existed. I can just pretend that he's nice and kind and loving, but if I met him face to face I might find I didn't like him at all.'

Morgan chuckled. 'You'll like him just fine, and that's a promise.'

'I don't want your promises. I just love the way you both think you can turn my life upside down at a moment's notice, expecting me to drop what I'm doing and rush off thousands of miles to be inspected, accepted or rejected. I have a very responsible job, and I enjoy my work, and the busy tourist season is just about to start. Do you expect me to leave Mr Drummond in the lurch? Well, I won't!'

'I'm sure if you explained the situation you'd find him very understanding,' Morgan suggested encouragingly.

'What! Tell him all about my private life?' Katriona's eyes glittered. 'Tell him that I have a father after all? That he's been a bit careless mislaying me for twenty years or so, but he has a little spare time on his hands now and would like to see if I have two heads or one. And I have other commitments ...'

'Oh, you mean Donald wanting to marry you. He'll keep,' Morgan offered with a grin. 'He's the faithful kind.'

'As opposed to your style of love 'em and leave 'em, I presume,' Katriona snapped angrily. 'You have no right to order my life and neither has Ross Carmichael, and for what it's worth neither has any other man.' She bent forward and snatched up the offending envelope and ripped it in two pieces and threw it under the table. '*I am not going to New Zealand!*'

She walked rapidly out of the hotel and was delighted to

see a taxi being paid off at the entrance. She got in and gave her address, and was pleased to see Morgan Grant come striding through the doors and down the entrance steps as she drove off. She had one glorious moment of tremendous satisfaction before she realised that she had behaved very badly, very badly indeed. But Morgan Grant was *too much*. Who did he think he was? He gave the impression that he was used to giving orders, used to getting his own way, and it was time he learned that everyone was not going to jump to attention each time he spoke. Katriona gave a small giggle. He did look so mad when he saw the taxi moving off!

All her life she had been taught not to be a nuisance, to be seen and not heard, to know that she was accepted only so long as her behaviour was acceptable. Why, even when her mother had offloaded her on to Ena when she was husband-hunting, she used to caution Katriona about outwearing her welcome. Behave yourself, baby, or Ena won't keep you and God knows what I'll do with you. All her life she had been made to fit in with other people's plans, to conform, to accept she was there on sufferance, and suddenly she was free. It was a heady experience. She felt as if she had thrown off the steel bands which repressed and restricted her. She could be herself. She felt like shouting and dancing in the streets.

Why had she been so pathetically emotionally crippled by the fact that she thought she had been illegitimate? How stupid she had been. Not that she had wanted to misbehave or be rude and impolite to everyone ... only some people. She laughed out loud and the taxi driver glanced over his shoulder and grinned at her. Really, she must control herself!

She paid the taxi off and gave him a brilliant smile and a handsome tip.

'Wish all my fares were like you, lady. It makes a nice change to carry someone cheerful. You meet a lot of moaners and groaners in this trade.'

Katriona went lightly up the stairs to her small apartment. She was busy searching her bag for her door key when she heard someone taking the stairs two at a time. Desperately she grabbed the key and thrust it into the lock.

'You could have waited for me. We could have shared a taxi.' Morgan Grant held the door open for her. He wasn't even out of breath.

'Blood and sand!' Katriona knew that as long as she lived she would never meet a more provoking man than this. She tried to hold in her sense of outrage and said coolly, 'Goodnight. I must thank you for the very nice dinner. Give my regards to my father when you see him.' She tried to close the door.

Morgan gently but firmly moved her inside and followed her in and closed the door behind him. 'Okay, the fun's over for tonight. When can I tell Ross to expect you?'

'You must have looked stupid launching yourself into a taxi and shouting "Follow that car".'

'I didn't do anything so dramatic. I had your home address from Donald, so I gave that to the cab driver. Sorry to disappoint you. I suppose you realise that this is the third time I've come running after you, and it will be the last. In the future if you want to see me you'll come running after me.'

Katriona gave him a venomous glance. 'I wouldn't hold my breath if I were you. You'll be waiting a long time ... say a lifetime or more.'

He leaned back against the closed door, his well defined lips parting in a smile which showed his teeth wonderfully white against his tanned face. 'The psychologist blokes reckon the harder a girl runs away from a man the more she fancies him.'

Katriona gasped as if she had been stung. 'Me fancy you? You conceited idiot! I ... I ... You're ...' She looked again and saw that he was grinning broadly. 'You're teasing me.'

'I am indeed,' he replied unrepentantly. 'You deserve it for your behaviour.'

Katriona stared at him; lean, tall, immaculately dressed

. . . so out of place in her rather shabby wee apartment. He appeared so much larger here than at the hotel. She would have rather kept him in ignorance of her pathetic accommodation. She was not ashamed of it. It was clean and it did not cost her very much, but she was sure he was not used to this style of living; she could tell that by the cut of his clothes and the expensive hotel he was staying at.

'How dare you follow me home? How dare you push your way into my apartment? If you don't leave immediately I'll ring the police and ask them to remove you. There's no need for you to stay here pestering me. You've had my answer—I'm not going to see my father. Anyway, *you* have no proof that he is my father.'

Morgan gave a great shout of laughter. 'Proof! I've got all the proof I need. You're the living image of him, and you're just as cantankerous as he is. Talk about a chip off the old block! I must be out of my skull trying to talk you into going to Evangeline. Sixty-three thousand acres wouldn't be big enough to hold you two comfortably!'

Katriona sat down abruptly. 'Sixty-three thousand acres! My father owns sixty-three thousand acres?'

Morgan took a careful survey of the room, then chose to sit on her bed which was not very well disguised as a settee. 'Yes. About a hundred square miles roughly. So you see it would be advisable for you to come and make his acquaintance.'

Colour flared in Katriona's cheeks. 'You're contemptible! Talking as if the fact that he was a wealthy man would make me reconsider my decision!'

Morgan waved his arm to include the apartment and its furnishings. 'You could hardly say you're living in the lap of luxury. Ross Carmichael provides better accommodation for his shearers than you've got here. And, Donald being the thrifty Scot that he is, I'm sure he would find you much more attractive with a well-heeled father.'

Katriona was so angry she could not speak. She burned to retaliate, to hurt as he had hurt her. Drawing herself to her full height, she said coldly, 'You may leave now. I'll never forgive you. You're cruel, insulting, ignorant and arrogant. When you get back to my father you can tell him you made an appalling error in tactics and because of your behaviour he'll never see me. I hope he'll dismiss you. It's what you deserve.'

'Why don't you come out and tell him yourself?' Morgan suggested lazily, not at all put out by her condemnation. 'You can hardly expect me to jeopardise my position by giving that message. I'm sure in the first excitement of seeing you he would be only too happy to grant any wish you mentioned.'

'Don't think I won't. It would be almost worth the trip to see you sent packing,' Katriona threw at him savagely.

'That's the girl, and so that you won't be out of pocket, I've written you another cheque. I'll look forward to seeing you.' Morgan got to his feet.

'Keep your cheque! If I ever go out there, I'll pay my own way. I'm completely independent, and I intend to stay that way. I will not be beholden to anyone. Can't you understand that?'

'I'm getting the message loud and clear.' The smile faded, leaving his face aloof and stern. 'Don't take too long about making up your mind. You've not asked anything about your father. You've been too preoccupied with your own feelings, and I can hardly blame you for that. Perhaps you think he's strong and healthy and in the prime of life. Just remember that he was a lot older than your mother when they married, and he's not had the best of health since she left him.'

'Is he a sick man?' Katriona was appalled at her pre-occupation with her own feelings.

'I shouldn't have mentioned it. Your father would be very annoyed to know I had.'

'You're not going to tell me?' Katriona asked in shocked tones.

'No, I'm not going to tell you. If you want to know you'll fly out and see him.' He stood up and put an envelope on the settee. 'There's the cheque, plus the directions how to get to Evangeline. I wouldn't take too long to decide about your trip. He could be quite desperately ill and you could arrive in a couple of months and be too late to meet him, and that would haunt you the rest of your life. Or you may get bowled over in the street and he would never get to meet you. He doesn't deserve that.'

With sudden awareness Katriona said angrily, 'You're just trying to make me feel guilty and ashamed. You're just trying to make me rush into a decision which I would regret. If my father was really seriously ill you would have said so immediately. That's emotional blackmail, and it won't work, and I think you're despicable to stoop to such methods. Even if I wanted to I couldn't leave my office at this particular time, I've given my word to Mr Drummond that I'll stay until he retires, and that may be in two months or six months or a year.'

'Come when you're ready . . .'

'I'll never be ready. I don't want any complications in my life. You go back to New Zealand and forget you ever met me, and I'll do my best to forget I've ever met you.'

Morgan stopped at the door and in one stride reached for her, his hands hard on her shoulders, 'You'll never forget me, Katriona Carmichael, that's a promise! And you'll never forget why I came; that out there in New Zealand you have a living, breathing father who needs someone to love more than most. Out there on Evangeline you'll have room to breathe, miles and miles of the most beautiful country in the world.' He shook her roughly. 'Don't be too stubborn, little Red. I'll go back and tell your father that he's got a daughter so like him it's ridiculous . . . an attractive, utterly feminine version of a proud, stubborn, bad-tempered old man.'

He laughed suddenly at her indignant expression and his hands dropped to his sides. 'I'll tell him I tried everything in the book. If I thought it would work I'd make wild passionate love to you and promise to marry you when you got back to New Zealand.'

'Don't you dare try!' Katriona backed away, her eyes

smouldering with rage.

Morgan laughed again. 'No, thanks. When Ross sent me he didn't order me to make this a suicide mission. See you at Evangeline.'

And he was gone.

Katriona stood in the same spot as he had left her, almost beside herself with temper, still feeling the pressure of his powerful hands on her shoulders. How conceited and arrogant he was! Did he think he only needed to make love to a girl, any girl, and she would chase him to the ends of the earth? Oh, Katriona wanted to shriek with rage, to have a tantrum, to somehow rid herself of all the unfamiliar emotions that Morgan Grant had triggered off in her neat and well planned existence. No man had the right to disturb her the way he had done.

No man had the right to literally take her breath away as Morgan Grant had done.

Gradually her fury lessened and her breathing became normal. She wandered over to her settee and sat down where he had been sitting and picked up the envelope he had left there. There was no doubt that this was his own handwriting, strong, bold and very masculine. Oh, yes, he was a man all right, from the tips of his well polished shoes to the thick dark curling hair on his very handsome head, and her tiny cramped apartment would never be the same now that he had been there. And she would never be the same ... she held the letter close to her, keeping it, holding it, treasuring it. Something of his.

She felt her cheeks burn as she realised where her thoughts were leading her. What if he had made love to her? Pain shot through her as she forced herself to be honest and admit she would have been wild with delight. Morgan Grant had some magic quality which drew people to him, and it was powerful magic. Look at the way Jeannie and Donald had been charmed by him, and Elspeth from the Lodge, and Shona and Morag, and silly, stupid, idiotic Katriona Carmichael. Glancing up, she caught sight of herself in the mirror, and it did not look like her at all. The girl in the mirror had a soft sweet mouth, and colour in her cheeks, and stars in her eyes. She looked like a girl in love ...

Katriona turned and flung herself down on the bed and cried as if her heart would break. She did not know why she was crying. Was she crying because she had found out she had a father? Or crying because she knew so little about him, and was scared of finding out more? Wasn't it better to be happy with a dream father rather than find the reality? He might not like her. He might be just like her mother and only want her in his life when it suited him. The tears continued to flow unchecked, and Katriona knew why. It was because Morgan Grant had gone. He had gone away laughing. He would laugh all the harder if he knew that a silly little nobody like her was crying her heart out in a shabby little bedsitter, and dreaming impossible dreams. Why, anyone as good-looking and personable as Morgan Grant could have any girl he liked ... he wouldn't waste a thought on her. She was just a job his employer had directed him to see to.

At last, Katriona lay quiet, completely exhausted. She was trying to picture him in her mind. Tall, virile and bronzed, an outdoor man with grey eyes that had a special far-seeing expression, grey eyes that could be laughing one moment and serious the next, and a shock of thick dark wavy hair, and his teeth were so white against his tanned face when he smiled ... and he smiled often.

Katriona finally pushed herself off her bed and went through to run a bath. It was foolish of her to waste time thinking about Morgan Grant, but she could not get him out of her mind. After her bath she had opened the envelope. Neatly printed on a card was his name and address: Morgan Grant, Evangeline Station, Lewis Pass Road, Private Bag, CHRISTCHURCH, and followed by the telephone Number 6820 Hanmer Springs. On the back of the card was written the cost of a first-class return air ticket plus a generous amount for expenses, and this matched the cheque. Also written were 'Cable when you're flying or ring when you arrive. See you soon. Morgan.'

'Oh, no, you won't, Morgan Grant,' she muttered out loud as she crawled in between the sheets. She made up her mind resolutely not to think about him. Restlessly she tossed and turned, always the same picture forming of him sitting in a huge jet, his long legs stretched out comfortably, and that attractive smile on his face. She would never see him again if she did not go to New Zealand. And she *wanted* to see him again. She couldn't go to New Zealand. He would think she was running after him. No, he wouldn't because he thought she was going to marry Donald, so she was safe going over there. No, she would never be safe going near Morgan Grant. She was infatuated by him and it would be okay when she got over it, then she could safely fly to Evangeline. What a romantic name! Oh, who cared about being safe? She must be out of her mind. She must mail that cheque back to him tomorrow. Then she would start saving her money. She had quite a bit saved, but it would take her another six months or more to save enough for a return ticket and a few nice clothes. Her heart pounded with excitement at the thought.

She tried fixing her mind on her father, but she had so little to go on, and Morgan would not be relegated to second place in her thoughts. She buried her head under her pillow. It was lucky that she had at least six months or longer to get him out of her system. Probably in a month's time she would hardly be able to remember what he looked like. In six months this whole episode would be forgotten.

She fell asleep.

Nearly nine months later Katriona sat tense in her seat as the huge jet lifted off with screaming engines on the first leg of her journey to New Zealand. She thought ruefully of her plan to forget about Morgan Grant in a month. There was no way that she could forget him. As the weeks and months passed she grew more and more angry with herself for being unable to drive him out of her thoughts. She had then thought perhaps she was making him too important, that if she let her mind travel back over his visit often enough it would lose its appeal and become so familiar it would be boring. It had not worked, and here she was feeling as if she was flying even a little ahead of the jet in a crazy desire to see him again.

She had not cabled that she was coming. She had no intention of ringing them up when she arrived in Christchurch. She was going to be completely independent and travel right out to the station under her own steam. She would not be beholden to them for anything, not the ticket nor even a ride from the airport. She had looked it up in a book on New Zealand, with maps and photographs, and discovered that Hanmer Springs, the nearest township to the station, was a holiday resort with ski fields, golf course, forest walks and horse riding as well as hot springs. There was not a lot of information about it, but enough for her to know that among all the visitors who came to swim in the sulphur pools for their health or to enjoy the other facilities she would go unnoticed.

She even had her ticket on a bus to take her there, although she had not booked any accommodation. She felt quite well organised. She could stay there for a few days and perhaps find out a little about the station before going there. She had tried to find out about it from the library, but although they seemed to have quite a lot of New Zealand material they had relatively little information about that area. From her map in the book of tourist resorts she could see where the station was on the Lewis Pass road, away up in the mountains, but that was all she could find out. She did not worry particularly, because she would learn all about it when she went there, if she liked it and if her father liked her; if not, what did it matter?

She had not slept much the week before she left. She had taken time out to visit Tiree and discuss her trip with Donald and Jeannie. She had not told them the whole truth, not the bit about her father ... that was too personal, and if he did not take to her, she would rather that they did not know she was rejected by her father as well as her mother. That would be too humiliating. They were so pleased for her and Donald promised to write at least once a week so that she would not feel homesick. It was very kind of him because it was very important to Katriona that regular letters would be arriving from Donald. Morgan Grant could not possibly suspect that she had any interest in him with Donald apparently so attentive.

She tried to relax but could not. The seats were comfortable, the food was delicious, the film entertaining, the stewardesses most thoughtful for her well-being, and even with all that unaccustomed luxury and attention she could feel the tension within her building up to fever pitch. After the stop-over in Singapore it was a direct flight to Auckland where she took her cases through Customs and boarded a smaller jet for Christchurch after a considerable wait.

As soon as she was seated she wanted to go to sleep. It was silly. She had not been able to sleep properly for weeks and the moment she arrived she was having a battle to keep her eyes open. The amicable lady in the seat next to her kept up a non-stop flow of conversation about her family and the conference to which she was travelling. Katriona wished she could take a polite interest, but kept drifting off to sleep only to wake with a fright a few seconds later. Suddenly she heard the name of her destination, Hanmer Springs.

She forced herself to concentrate. 'You're going to Hanmer Springs, did you say? So am I. Isn't that a coincidence?'

The lady was enchanted. 'Incredible! I wonder if the booking office knew and put us together deliberately ... oh, no, that's highly unlikely. How are you getting out there from Christchurch? Are you going to the nurses' conference too? By the way, my name is Sylvia Furness. And yours?'

'Katriona Carmichael. I'm not going to your conference, I'm just going for a short holiday. I'm going up in a bus.' She fished into her traveller's wallet and produced the ticket. 'Are you travelling on the same bus?'

Sylvia Furness shook her head emphatically. 'No. Friends are picking me up at the airport. Say, they'll have room for one more. You don't want to hang around town for hours. Have you got much luggage?'

Bewildered at the turn of events, Katriona shook her head. 'It's very good of you, but I wouldn't like to put you to any trouble.'

'No trouble at all,' Sylvia Furness assured her. 'We'll cancel your bus reservation and you'll be in Hanmer hours ahead of the bus. I'll organise the whole thing.'

Katriona felt it required too much effort to argue. Sylvia Furness was very kindhearted, but she much preferred to keep to her own arrangements. Unwillingly she gave way and then gave up the struggle to stay awake.

'Wake up, my dear. We're coming in to land. Fasten your seat belt. There's the Southern Alps. See out there ... that's right ... aren't they a glorious sight? Fantastic day. You've slept like a baby.'

Katriona felt as if she had been drugged. She managed to take in some of the beauty of the snow-capped mountains and the fields laid out below, and then they landed. Feeling distinctly crumpled, she followed Sylvia Furness across the tarmac to the lounge, and drifted off to sleep as soon as she was seated.

'Wake up, Katriona. Meet Bunty and Judy. Your bus seat has been cancelled and you're travelling with us. Let's go. I've got your cases sorted out.'

Katriona smiled wanly at the two ladies she had been introduced to and followed them out to a car in the parking lot and was no sooner seated than she was fading off to sleep again.

She heard Sylvia say, 'Poor child. Jet lag, I suppose. Pretty wee thing. Such a coincidence ...'

'Comfort stop.' Sylvia was shaking her roughly. 'We're at Culverdun. Out you hop. Toilets over there and we'll be in the tea-rooms along there. See? Now don't go back to sleep, a hot cup of tea is what you need. I've already woken you once. Really, you do take chances! We could have been a gang of white slavers. You haven't a clue where you are, have you?'

Katriona shook her head and picked up her bag, and walked to the toilets. The afternoon sun had struck her like a blast from an oven, and she was glad to strip off her jacket and splash her face in the cold water. She repaired her make-up and combed her tangled curls. Sylvia was right, she felt better, but she needed that cup of tea. Slinging her bag over her shoulder and dangling her jacket over her arm, she started along the street towards the tea-rooms.

A small pick-up truck swung into the curb beside her, and she gave it a casual inspection, then a more intent look as the name painted on the door almost leapt out at her: 'Evangeline'. Enchanted, she stared at it. That truck came from her father's station! Suddenly she felt she was being watched and looked inside the cab of the truck. She looked directly into the cool grey eyes of *Morgan Grant*.

She turned as if to run ... but there was nowhere to go. She was in his territory now. Maybe he had not recognised her? After all, he wasn't expecting her. Oh, yes, he knew who she was. He came striding round the front of the truck towards her. Tall and lean, lithe and brown, he appeared much bigger than she remembered him.

She swallowed nervously, her head lifted up defiantly. If only she could get her breath properly, she'd handle this situation without trouble.

'Good afternoon, Mr Grant,' she stammered a little breathlessly.

He stopped in front of her, his eyes lit with some secret amusement. 'Good afternoon, Katriona Carmichael. You sure took your time coming. Allow me to welcome you formally to New Zealand.' He shook hands with her briskly. 'Now where's your luggage? How are you travelling?'

'In that powder blue station-wagon. I'm with three ladies who went into the tea-room for a cup of tea.'

'Right. Get in the cab. It's just lucky I came in to pick up a dog. I'll go and get the car key from your friend and sling your luggage in the back. We'll be home in half an hour.'

Things were getting out of control, Katriona decided. 'You'll do nothing of the sort! I'm going to Hanmer Springs. I'm going to stay there for a few days.'

'Have you booked in?' He whipped the question at her.

She shook her head.

'Well, you haven't a hope in hell of getting a bed there. I was there last week and they said everything is booked out with two big conferences.'

'But . . .' Katriona protested.

'But . . . nothing. Even if you could get six beds you wouldn't be staying there. What are you trying to do? Humiliate your father? How long do you think it would take the district to learn that Ross Carmichael's daughter was staying there? Hop in, I haven't got time to mess about.'

Katriona obeyed him without speaking again. She slammed the truck door angrily as he headed towards the tea-rooms. She was surprised to find herself trembling. In a way it was a relief to have the decision to go to the station taken out of her hands. There was no way out now. Immediately following the relief came the swift anger and resentment at his high-handed action. He had taken her arrival so calmly, as if he had known to the day and the minute when she would arrive in this wee country town. He could have no idea of the struggle she had gone through trying to make up her mind whether to travel thousands of miles to see him again . . . because that was in essence why she had come. Yes, of course it had been because she wanted to see her father, that had been terribly important to her, but it was also very important to her to get Morgan Grant in proper perspective. He was ruining her carefully planned life, he invaded her thoughts, and even her dreams. And she *resented* it.

She hoped he would not be able to find Sylvia, and would have to come crawling back and ask her help. Just then he came out of the doorway and down the steps with Sylvia positively oozing all over him. He winked as he went past as if he knew what she had been thinking. It did not improve her mood.

He threw the cases in the back, thanking Sylvia with charming old-world courtesy, then came round and slid in beside Katriona.

Sylvia leaned in through the open window. 'Do you think he's a white slaver? If he is, ask him to come back for me!' She laughed delightedly and waved them away.

They drove in silence for a while. Katriona was furious. No man had the right to disturb her the way he had done—storming into her life and out of it again. She flicked a sideways glance at him. He was only a man. Nothing special about him. He was really very ordinary ... good-looking, but ordinary. A week or two in the same house and she would probably find him dreadfully boring.

His bare bronzed arm touched hers and she flinched as if she had received an electric shock. Maybe it would take three weeks to discover how boring he could be!

CHAPTER THREE

KATRIONA stared out of the truck window at the passing landscape with unseeing eyes. She was aware only of the close proximity of Morgan Grant and the rising tide of panic that threatened to overwhelm her at the thought of meeting her father.

What a fool she had been to let Morgan Grant precipitate her into this situation! All the joy and excitement had drained away leaving her exhausted and frightened. She just felt so tired. If only she had had a few days to recover from her trip she would have been better equipped both mentally and physically to meet her father.

Oh, why hadn't she written to say she was arriving? It was stupid to be thrown on his doorstep without warning. It was all Morgan Grant's fault. Oh, she wished she was wearing a dress. A dress was so much more feminine. A man would expect to see his daughter in a dress ... that is if he were meeting her for the first time. Well, wouldn't he? She ran a finger down the crease of her well-cut and smoothly fitting denim pants then touched her expensive peach-coloured silk overshirt, outlining the exquisite embroidery, glad in her heart that it was delightfully feminine. Her matching denim jacket and cap lay on the seat beside her.

She picked up the cap in her hand and twirled it around nervously. She was glad she had the cap. She brushed a stray curl back into place and rammed it on the back of her head. She knew it gave her a jaunty carefree appearance, a false air of bravado. She flicked a glance across at Morgan and found him watching her with a cool calculating stare. He nodded a little grimly and returned his attention to his driving.

Resentfully Katriona waited for him to speak. It was

almost as if he had summed up all her possibilities in one long slow measured look, then transferred his thoughts to some more interesting project. At last she could not bear the suspense. She wanted to know what his conclusions were.

'Well? Did I pass?' Her voice reflected her anger.

There was a long pause as if Morgan had forgotten her existence altogether and had to gather his thoughts together before replying. Infuriated, Katriona realised that he was doing it deliberately, playing the dominating male part to make her feel insignificant ... and it must not work.

He did not look at her, but she saw a muscle in his tanned cheek twitch and the beginnings of a smile on his lips. 'You'll do.'

That was deliberate too. What a nerve he had! 'You do *work* for my father?' Katriona asked, a cutting edge in her voice as she attempted to show him his place.

'In a manner of speaking,' his laughter mocked her as if he guessed her purpose. 'You mean, seeing I work for your father, I should know him well enough to be able to guess his reaction to your sudden arrival?'

It had not been what Katriona had meant, but she was anxious to know the answer. 'Well?'

The muscle in his cheek twitched again. 'That would be very presumptuous of me ... a mere workman ... to guess at your father's intentions.'

'Very amusing,' Katriona said with heavy sarcasm. Oh, yes, he had known she was trying to put him down and she deserved his remark, but it did not make her fond of him. She hated him, with his mock humility and his arrogant good looks.

'Can you drive? I mean do you possess a driver's licence?'

'No, I haven't,' Katriona replied shortly.

'We'll have to remedy that. I'll get one of the boys to teach you.'

'Why should you?' Katriona demanded.

'I presume you want to make yourself useful while you're

here. Evangeline is fully mechanised, so you'll be a dead loss if you can't drive.'

'If my f ... er ... Mr Carmichael will arrange for me to have lessons if he thinks it necessary,' Katriona replied somewhat pointedly, her small chin lifting defiantly.

Morgan laughed. 'Oh, Ross leaves most of the running of Evangeline to me these days. He can't manage to do too much on the farm.'

Katriona was silent. So that was why he was so arrogant, and why he had so much authority. Her poor father was ill and old, and Morgan Grant had taken over and pushed him into the background. Her back stiffened and her lips tightened aggressively. He might be able to bully a tired frail old man, but he need not think he would get very far ordering her around! She was glad she had come. Why, he had even used the station cheque book as if it was his own. She leaned back in her seat and closed her eyes. She needed time to sort her ideas out. She needed time ...

'Evangeline.' Morgan's voice seemed to come from a tremendous distance. Katriona fought to throw off the heaviness of sleep.

'Thought you wouldn't like to arrive in the yard asleep on my shoulder. Might create the wrong impression.'

The words stung her like an electric shock. She suddenly became aware of her position, and jerked herself upright. Down below her was a small lake, brilliantly blue, sparkling in the gold of the late March sunlight, fringed with green reeds and flax bushes ... incredibly beautiful.

It disappeared from view as they wound their way up a steep hill, then suddenly reappeared. A jet boat sped across the surface of its almost indigo waters.

'We swim there throughout the summer. Can you water-ski?' Morgan had slowed down for her to have a closer view of the lake. 'Horseshoe Lake. Quite a little beauty, isn't it?'

Katriona was enchanted by the fabulous jewel-like setting of the green-fringed lake.

'That's Evangeline over there.'

She gasped as she gazed across the wide gully to the

plateau beyond. Surely her father's station must be the most beautiful place in the whole world. How long had she slept? She remembered, as they left that country town, the flat, sun-scorched land. Now she was gazing at Evangeline, high up in the mountain pass. Nestled in the tawny hills, set out attractively in a green oasis of pine and poplar plantations, were the brown-stained farm building and the white homestead and cottages, all green-roofed and drenched in glorious sunlight.

She stared again at the lake, her eyes moving across the rough gully with gorse and broom up to the well set out homestead and buildings, beyond to the tawny tussock hills, and higher yet to the blue-purple-shadowed mountain peaks.

'How do you like it?' Morgan demanded. 'Worth the trip?'

Only then did Katriona become aware that he had stopped the truck to give her this perfect unrestricted view, and also became aware of the searching perceptive grey eyes watching alertly for her reaction.

'Who could fail to be impressed? Fantastic. Have you lived here all your life?'

'Not all of it ... most of it.'

'Then I think you've been very fortunate.'

'You could have been here too.' He started the truck and moved off down the sweeping curve of the hill towards the station. As they turned the corner near the foot of the hill she saw a huge river, jade green in the shadow of the towering bluffs, and a river of molten silver where the sun struck it.

'Oh, how very beautiful! Does it belong to the station?'

'That's the Hope River. It's a boundary between us and the next station ... Hope Valley station.'

Around the next corner Morgan swung the truck off the main road and stopped by a mailbox, collected a parcel, then moved on up the road towards the homestead. He left a cloud of dust behind him as he gunned the truck across the flat stretch of gravel road, then swept up a sharp rise and round a small bluff and into a huge yard.

Katriona thought it looked a bit like a village square with cars and farm trucks and machinery about, gas pumps and so many buildings she would never learn what they were for. Several young men were standing by a car, stripped to the waist, their well muscled bodies, deeply tanned, turned gold in the setting sun. They were drinking beer from bottles with obvious enjoyment.

Morgan sketched them a casual salute. 'That's the shearers just finished a day's crutching. They sure deserve their beer tonight.'

He passed them and swung around in a wide curve to park in front of the homestead. 'Come on.' He lifted her cases out.

Katriona slid from her seat and followed him to the gate, then stopped, half in admiration for the house and surroundings and half in sheer terror at the coming meeting. There was plenty of reason to stop and stare by the wrought iron gate. The house looked, from a commanding position, over the Hope River and station flats, down to the main Lewis Pass road. Graceful mature silver birch trees made a fitting entrance to a lovely home. Katriona saw Morgan disappear through large ranch-slider doors and knew she would have to follow him. She walked along the neat cement path; appreciating the green sweep of the well-kept terraced lawns and garden, the colourful profusion of flowers and shrubs and the sheer elegance of the superb standard roses blooming in all their glory, which formed a guard of honour each side of the path from the front gate to the door.

There was no sign of Morgan, nor anyone else, when Katriona reached the huge glass doors, so she stopped, wondering whether to go in or not. She peeped in and was instantly captured by the warm welcoming aspect of the attractively furnished room. This living room had been planned with excellent taste and loving care to a perfect blend of the old and new, from the modern richness of the deep pile carpet and comfortable easy chairs and couch to the beauty of the highly polished brasses and the dominating majesty of the centuries-old grandfather clock. Certainly the high point of the room would be the perfectly proportioned heavy kauri table, the matchless gleam of its polished surface reflecting the glowing colours of a pottery bowl of nasturtiums arranged with careful casualness.

Intrigued, Katriona inched a little further into the room, admiring the huge wide open fireplace and high old-fashioned mantelpiece, then saw beyond the cascading pot-plants on the room divider a magnificent modern kitchen, gleaming and shining, the model of efficiency, the snow-white curtains moving gently in the soft early evening breeze.

Suddenly a sadness that was a physical pain caught at her heart with tearing intensity, making her turn from the solid warmth and invitation of the room to the cool perfumed fragrance of the garden. Tears filled her eyes as she tried to fight off the bitter knowledge that all this beauty and security could have been hers. She could have grown up here, she could have swung in the swing that hung from the lower limb of the silver birch by the gate, as a baby she could have sat in the lovingly preserved colonial high-chair in the living-room ... she could have called this wonderful place her home.

A shrill cry made her hurriedly brush away her tears, and to her incredible delight she saw a peacock with its tail-feathers spread wide, displaying the iridescent blue and green glory with justified pride. Open-mouthed, Katriona watched it strut and parade in and out between the roses with a proprietorial air, until an extremely large white cat bounded on to the lawn with tail switching, followed shortly by an aggressive tortoiseshell cat, and the ensuing battle put the peacock to flight.

Morgan came out of the house and down the steps in a hurry. 'They're up at the new house.'

Katriona caught his arm. 'There was a peacock in the garden—a real peacock in among the roses! It's flown away.'

The frown on Morgan's face cleared as he gazed down at the bright awed look in her blue eyes. 'It's okay. There are a pair of them here. You're not seeing things. They range free. We don't cage any bird if we can help it, except the kea, and I doubt he'd fly away even if he wasn't caged. He lives like royalty on the biscuits the tourists feed him. Come along. Ross is up at the new house and Nivvy has just taken him up his afternoon tea, so we're in luck.'

An appalling thought struck Katriona as she turned back to the open door and saw the bowl of orange and yellow nasturtiums ... a woman's touch, without doubt.

'Nivvy? Is she your wife?' She was pleased that her voice sounded only a little breathless as she hurried to follow him down the path.

'No, she isn't. She's my housekeeper.' He held the gate open for her. 'Do I *look* married?' He was insulted.

'No, but they're the worst sort.' Katriona giggled as she got back in the truck, although she knew it was no laughing matter. The knowledge of how shattered she had felt to think Morgan was married gave her an idea of the depth of her feeling for him. She backed away from that discovery.

'That would be the voice of experience talking?' Morgan questioned.

'Of course!' Katriona replied without truth. 'What do you mean by tourists feeding the kea? Where is the new house? Whose new house?'

He swung the truck almost full circle and drove through an open cyclone gate by a barn filled with hay. 'There are the deer ... see? This was one of the first deer farms in New Zealand and the deer park was opened to give the public a chance to see the deer.'

Katriona was staring round-eyed at the deer in the enclosure which ran from the gravel road they were driving on back across the fields to a stream and the plantation beyond. An enormous stag stood at the edge of the trees, his head thrown back in classic stance as he gave his deep, full-throated roar.

'You're lucky to be here for the roar ... that's the mating

season ... March, April, May.'

'You farm deer?' Katriona wanted to be sure she had it correct. 'How many? Where are they?'

'We've over a thousand now. We run them up on Mount Kakapo,' Morgan explained as he waved to two small boys playing with a Hereford calf by a big pine in front of another farm cottage.

'Head shepherd's house.'

Katriona gulped. 'My father owns a mountain?'

'Several,' Morgan answered casually. 'Although we call them hills.'

'I'll call them mountains,' Katriona promised him.

Morgan grinned, 'I'm sure you will. You'd be just the sort to make a mountain out of a molehill, let alone an ordinary hill. There's your father's brain-child—his new house. You'd better like it ... God knows what he paid the architect who designed it!'

'I'll like it,' Katriona interrupted with a swift fierce loyalty which surprised her. Poor old crippled man, enjoying a little pleasure from building himself a house while this domineering Morgan was critical! Naturally she would side with her father. Together they'd put Morgan Grant where he belonged. A little of her certainty drained away as Morgan followed the narrow twisting road through the trees for a short distance, then emerged on to a clearing in front of the new house.

'Follow me,' Morgan commanded as he leapt nimbly down and went up the wide smooth steps of the new house with confidence.

Katriona followed him on shaky legs. Her father might be getting a little pleasure, but he was building a lot of house ... it was a mansion, perfectly proportioned, and artistically designed to blend in with the landscape. It was still in the raw unfinished state, but it spoke of elegance and charm, not to mention luxury.

'Wait here,' Morgan instructed her. 'Your father will probably be in his office. It's almost finished. He has it furnished, and the kitchen is almost complete.'

'I don't want a builder's report!' Katriona spat out the words.

'Sorry, I am rambling on. Naturally you're nervous ... It will be all right, little Red.'

Katriona's head came up and her eyes sought his for re-assurance, but found something else ... *pity!* Fear clawed at her throat, and she grabbed his arm. 'You never did say what sort of a man my father was. Tell me now or I'll walk out of here!'

Aware that she was on the edge of panic, Morgan spoke quietly. 'Your father is a fine man. He'll do me to cross the river with ... Do you know what that means, little Red? Here, where the rivers run deep and swift, two men can cross more safely than one, but you virtually trust your partner with your life.' He hesitated as if to add something and thought better of it, turned and left the room rapidly.

Katriona wandered over to the huge floor-to-ceiling picture windows which gave her a panoramic view of the station. She could see the head shepherd's house, the deer park, and further away the homestead in the trees. She could see the Lewis Pass road snaking its way past the front gate. She hugged her arms across her chest, feeling cold in spite of the obvious warmth of the day. Progress was being made on a swimming pool and barbecue area to her left ...

'Good afternoon! May I help you?'

Katriona came round with a jerk to find a pleasant-looking dark-haired woman wearing a sun-frock watching her from the doorway.

'Oh, no ... thanks. I'm just waiting to see Mr Car-michael,' Katriona replied nervously.

'That's okay, then.' The woman gave her a warm smile. 'I'm Janet Niven, the housekeeper. Does he know you're here?'

'Yes, thank you. Morgan Grant brought me, and he's gone to find him.' Katriona was acutely aware that she had to clench her teeth to keep them from chattering.

'If Morgan is looking after you, I've no need to worry. I'm just going to put on afternoon tea, so you've arrived at the right time.' Mrs Niven gave her a friendly nod and then left.

Morgan was not looking after her, Katriona thought resentfully. He had been gone absolutely ages. What could be happening? Perhaps her father was angry at her for arriving unannounced ... worse still, perhaps he no longer wanted to see her. Perhaps she would be sent away ignominiously. She flung back her hair in a defiant gesture and slammed her cap back on as this thought struck her. She *would* not care. She had a little money left and her return ticket. She was nobody's charity child. She could look after herself, had been doing so for years. In fact she would leave right now. If he did not want a daughter, then she did not want a father. She had managed perfectly well without a father for twenty-one years.

She wheeled around and started back to tell Mrs Niven that she was leaving, and met Morgan.

'Oh, Katriona, I was just coming to get you. Sorry to have taken so long ...'

'Don't apologise,' Katriona snapped furiously. 'I was a fool to come. I don't know how I could have been so foolish!'

'Hey, girl, don't get mad at the old man before you meet him. Don't be scared.'

'I'm not scared,' Katriona hissed. That was the truth, because she was beyond being scared and was almost petrified.

Morgan caught her elbow and somehow propelled her up a short flight of steps, and flung open a door in front of her. He gave her a slight push of encouragement as she passed him and closed the door behind her.

Aghast, Katriona realised that Morgan had abandoned her, not even stopping to smooth the way with an introduction. She *hated* him! Morgan Grant was a mean, miserable, unfeeling beast. She glanced around her, noting that she was in some sort of an office, with book-lined shelves and leather chairs. Slowly she lifted her eyes to the desk in the corner, and then to the tall silver-haired man leaning against that desk. He was smoking a pipe and seemed to be scrutinising her carefully. He showed no sign that her precipitate arrival had disturbed him.

He levered himself off the desk and walked towards her, his hand extended. 'Well, Miss Carmichael, Miss Katriona Carmichael, it's a real pleasure to meet you at last.'

Katriona shook hands automatically. 'Thank you,' she muttered, feeling utterly ridiculous.

'Now, if you'd be so kind as to take this chair here, I'll sit myself down at my desk and we'll proceed to get to know each other slowly. I'm sure Mrs Niven will make an appearance at any moment with afternoon tea. Or maybe, having travelled a long way, you would care for something a little stronger? Sherry? Whisky?'

'No, thank you, a cup of tea will be fine, thank you.' Katriona felt that she was in a state of shock. Nothing was as she had imagined it. Somehow she had built up a picture of a lonely, sick old man, heavily built, partly crippled. He could have been in a wheelchair, a little dazed and bewildered from being pushed around by an aggressive, impatient young man, namely Morgan Grant. Nothing could have been further from the truth, and she was hastily trying to adjust herself to the changed circumstances.

Her father was a tall, lean, athletically built and well dressed man, eminently capable of looking after himself. He had a strong masculine face, almost ruthless, tanned to mahogany, with bushy eyebrows hooding steel-blue eyes.

'Did you have a good trip out from Scotland, Miss Carmichael?' He stretched back comfortably in his expensive swivel chair, casually crossing his long legs.

'Yes, thank you,' Katriona stammered politely. She was sitting bolt upright in her chair, knees together, hands primly folded on her lap, almost as if she was being interviewed for a job. Why should she be so much on the defensive? She did not know why; just that she was. Somehow his polite, polished manner was rapidly reducing her nerves to pulp.

The door opened and Mrs Niven came in bearing an

attractive afternoon tea on a tray. 'Will I pour for you, Ross?'

'Yes, of course. Unless Miss Carmichael would care to do the honours?'

Until they both looked at her, Katriona did not realise that it was a question. She shook her head emphatically. 'No. Thank you.'

Her mind was a chaotic whirl of impressions, sliding and jumping together. First and foremost was the fact that her father had said it was a pleasure to meet her. It was quite obvious that he lied. He was bored to his back teeth. Secondly, he was treating her like a visitor ... no, job applicant. He had more warmth in his tone when he spoke to his housekeeper than when he spoke to her. Katriona watched Mrs Niven pour the tea and hand her father a cup, then the sugar bowl. She started to do a long slow burn. She watched him smile at Mrs Niven as he helped himself to a freshly baked cheese scone from the plate she offered him. The long slow burn started to speed up, almost as if she was getting her second wind after a long and gruelling race.

He could be casual and relaxed, could he? So, she could be too! Deliberately she took off her jaunty Dutch cap and dropped it on the floor, then ran her fingers through her red-gold hair and patted it into shape, before taking her cup from Mrs Niven.

'Why, how exceedingly kind of you, Mrs Niven. That's exactly how I like my tea ... not too weak, not too strong.' Katriona smiled sweetly at the housekeeper. 'Those scones look absolutely delicious, may I try one?'

'Certainly. Kind of you to say so, Miss ... er ... Miss ...'

'Katriona,' Katriona offered with the same sweet smile, taking a scone.

'Katriona,' Mrs Niven grabbed gratefully for the name. 'Now I'll leave you two to enjoy yourselves.' She left the room hurriedly.

Katriona placed her cup and saucer on the small occasional table beside her, eased herself back in the large leather chair, and casually crossed her legs before regaining her tea. Her eyes narrowed slightly as she looked across the broad expanse of the desk at her father.

'A pleasant woman, Mrs Niven. Is it difficult to get staff out here in the back of beyond?' It was a phrase she had borrowed from her companion on the plane, Sylvia.

For an instant she saw a hint of admiration in those cold blue eyes. Good enough. She had hardly expected him to gather her in his arms muttering emotional greetings, but surely there was somewhere between that and his present stance. The gleam in his eye showed he was not unaware of her tactics. Morgan had called him good and kind. *Kind!* Someone to cross the river with! Katriona felt that at this moment if they were in a good deep river he would probably hold her head under the water, the way cruel people did to stray kittens.

'No, we don't find it terribly difficult to get staff here or to hold them. We're a bit isolated, but much depends on how you treat staff, and of course how you pay them. We've always had a good track record.'

Katriona was tempted to say that she'd like a position on the staff, say that she'd heard there was a vacancy for an appointment of daughter of the house. She bit her lip and firmly repressed the desire to be sarcastic. 'You have a beautiful home here, Mr Carmichael. I love the use you're making of natural wood ... such warm tones ... and those panels are superb.' It hurt, having to call him Mr Carmichael, to be so formal, when Mrs Niven could comfortably call him Ross.

'Yes. I'm justifiably proud of it. Pity I didn't have it completed before your arrival. Still, Morgan said he put your cases in at the homestead, you'll be comfortable there. Traditionally that's the manager's house. I was living there when I married your mother.'

'So you believe I'm your daughter?' Katriona turned her attention to her scone and tea, feeling she could not watch him at this crucial moment.

There was such a lengthy silence on the other side of the

desk that eventually she was forced to look across at the tough old man.

He met her gaze quite steadily, almost indifferently. 'Yes, you are my daughter. Morgan was convinced of it when he returned. You made quite an impression on him, I gather, and as far as women go he's a very hard man to impress.'

'You flatter me,' Katriona replied smoothly. Her thoughts ran riot, as she thought of Morgan coaxing her to come here, when he must have known she was not wanted. No wonder he threw her into this lion's den and went rushing off! She vowed to herself that she intended to make a much more lasting impression on him the next time she saw him.

'I wasn't flattering you, only stating a fact. I would have said he was completely immune to any woman's attractions. Up till now none of them have managed to make a dent in his protective armour, and believe me, plenty have tried.'

'I have no doubt of it,' Katriona replied with vigour. 'He's a very conceited young man.'

'And you have a very sharp tongue, young lady,' her father spoke sharply.

Katriona grinned. Strike one! He doesn't like his favourite young man criticised. Well, he'd have to put up with a lot of that if she stayed around here.

Almost reluctantly her father smiled back at her, then his expression returned to a bitter brooding one. She felt if she could break through that tough steel barrier of indifference which he had erected around himself, she could learn to enjoy her father. She sighed deeply. She doubted if it were worth the effort, and it would take a mighty effort to gain recognition for herself as a person, and then as a daughter. He had no reason to look on her with joy. He had not wanted a daughter all these years the way she had wanted a father.

She could not blame him for not wanting to become involved in her life. She was a complete stranger. Her mother by her behaviour years ago had destroyed any hope of their embarking on a good relationship. It was all such a pity. He could only feel anger and bitterness for the hurts he had suffered long ago, and it was natural to associate her with her mother. Poor man, maybe he was wondering if she really had come to grab for the pot of gold at the end of the rainbow, the rich man's daughter trying to cash in on her inheritance.

The thought was unbearable. Placing the empty cup on the table very carefully, Katriona stood up. Then she saw her cap on the floor and grabbing it she stuck it on at a crazy angle before facing her father.

'You said it was a real pleasure to meet me at last, but you don't look pleased. You look completely indifferent. I don't blame you.' Katriona's small slender figure had a certain dignity as she drew herself to her full height, even if her voice was slightly husky with emotion.

She tried to swallow away the lump in her throat, and kept on speaking. 'I can say with all honesty that it was a pleasure to meet you. All my life I've wanted and needed a real father. I've had several substitute ones, and sometimes they were good to me, but they were substitutes. You see, all my life I've believed I was illegitimate. I know in this day and age it shouldn't count, but with me it did. I must have only been six or seven when I overheard two teachers discussing my report, saying something about a poor something background and no father image. I know now they didn't mean what I thought they did, but I felt crushed and humiliated, and I never grew up enough to put it behind me.'

Her father leaned forward in his chair 'Look, I'm sorry if I gave you the wrong impression. I do apologise . . .'

'Don't apologise,' Katriona interrupted fiercely. 'You have *nothing* to apologise for. You didn't even know that I existed. I haven't come here to cause you trouble, I was just curious. And Morgan said you wanted to see me too. Surely you can allow me that much . . . to see you, to speak with you, to see where you live, where I would have lived . . . I want nothing from you. I think we could have been friends. I think we could have been a . . . a comfort to each other all these years, but my mother's actions have effectively washed out any chance of that. You can't look at me without feeling pain and resentment. I was stupid to have come. I'll find Morgan and get him to take me to the nearest town. Goodbye.'

She walked swiftly from the room without looking back. She half ran down the steps, then set off in the direction of the homestead. She was burning up with all sorts of emotions—sadness, disappointment, anger, resentment, and most of all indignation at Morgan Grant. He must have known what her reception was going to be, and he had just pushed her in and cleared off. Well, she would let him have a piece of her mind before she made him drive her to Hanmer Springs. How dared he place her in this impossible situation!

She marched up the path to the homestead and into the kitchen. Ignoring Mrs Niven's surprised expression, she demanded, 'Where will I find Morgan Grant?'

'He's away at the moment. They're having some trouble down by Horseshoe Lake and he's gone over to give a hand. He should be up in about an hour with the cattle. You've had a long tiring trip, you must be very weary. Morgan has put your cases in your room and I've made up the bed. He said you'll be staying for a while. How about a nice shower to freshen yourself up, and a wee rest?'

'You're very kind,' Katriona could barely control her voice, 'but Morgan gave you false information. I'm leaving immediately, so he'll have to carry my cases out again. Now is there a short cut to where he's working?'

Mrs Niven hesitated for a moment, but after a searching glance at Katriona's strained expression, she said with a hint of compassion in her voice, 'Take my car—the red Cortina, here's the keys.'

Katriona shook her head, feeling the tears threaten at such kindness. 'Sorry. It's very good of you to offer me the car, but I can't drive.' She could see the long road out to the front gate, and the twisting, turning main highway disappearing behind the far hill, and felt she just could not walk that distance. Yet she must get to Morgan. It was a matter of extreme urgency. She could not be here when her father came back from the new house. Oh, Morgan Grant was going to pay for what he'd done to her!

'Please, there must be a short cut?' she asked almost desperately.

Mrs Niven looked troubled. 'I'd love to help you. Could I get one of the boys to take you down? Or Ross himself would, I'm sure ...' She stopped, seeing Katriona's expression. 'All right, my dear. See the woolshed over there ... no, that's the cookhouse and men's quarters. To your right ... yes, see the sheepyards ... good. I've heard the men say they can drop down over that bank behind the yards by the poplars, and get across to the Lake, but I've never been that way myself. Look, there's a swamp and they're handling wild cattle. If you'd wait ...'

But Katriona was not waiting, she was running down the path and across the yard. She battled to open a heavy iron gate only to find it padlocked. Angrily she threw herself over it, badly barking a shin-bone in the process. Oh, Morgan Grant was going to pay ... and pay! She ran along the side of an enormous building which was obviously the woolshed, then over another gate, past a small neat building and then over to the towering line of poplars behind the yards.

Standing on the edge of the terrace which overlooked a bank of tangled undergrowth and trees, she stopped and stared across to the large scrub-covered flat through which meandered a stream on its way to the Hope River. It looked wild, rugged, rough country and she felt slightly daunted. Then a stockman's whistle split the quiet evening air and across the gully from the picturesque Horseshoe Lake came the sound of dogs barking and cattle roaring. Morgan Grant. Immediately her temper flared again. A few wild cattle and a swamp would not keep her from that man. Even if the path was guarded by fire-eating dragons and peppered with volcanoes, she would still take it, she vowed extravagantly. Oh, Morgan Grant was going to get his due when she reached him! His good looks and superficial charm would not save him.

With that thought in mind she plunged headlong down
what she took to be a well-used sheep track, and the
shortest possible route to that wretched man. The track
was steeper than she expected. Stumbling and falling down
the steep incline, she kept losing her footing and, bruised
and muddied, she arrived at the bottom angrier and more
determined than ever to face up to Morgan. The trail became worse and she was soon surrounded by bush ferns,
dead and decaying windblown willows overgrown with
vines, wild gooseberry bushes and swamp.

No thought of turning back entered her head. Jumping
from knob to knob, sometimes missing her objective, she
emerged on firmer ground with her well-cut jeans liberally
coated with slime and mud. Dishevelled, with her long red
hair strewn damply across her determined face, she
marched on like some slender avenging angel, her hair
glinting in the last rays of the setting sun and her vivid blue
eyes fixed on the tussock hill by the lake, each bump and
hurt adding fuel to her anger.

The rocky river bed was strewn with briar and thorny
matagouri bushes which tore and scratched her clothes
and bare hands, but she was getting closer to the sound of
the bellowing cattle and barking dogs.

Suddenly, out of the stony creekbed, the cattle burst
from the scrub, the mob of long-horned animals heading
directly towards where Katriona stood with no tree or fence
for miles. Pale-faced, she watched the dogs vainly trying to
head the charge, and was vaguely aware that several horse-
men also appeared on the scene, but they were too far
away to do her much good. She was sick with dismay as she
realised how stupid she was and what danger she was in as
the maddened cattle slashed at the dogs with their horns.
Their red eyes and frothing mouths warned her they were
very dangerous. They were so close to her now that she
could see the steam rising from their sweating flanks. She
wanted to run, but there was nowhere to run to . . .

'Katriona!'

She turned towards the shout and saw a rider on a magnificent grey horse come racing towards her. Cutting fast between her and the leading bull, he wheeled about and leaning from the saddle swept her into his arm, spurring his horse to safety. Katriona could only cling to him, feeling herself pinioned to his chest by the steel-like grip of his arm. He hoisted her up in front of him on the saddle and she could feel his heart pounding in tune with her own.

'You okay?'

Katriona nodded, keeping her head buried in his jacket, ashamed to let him see just how frightened she had been.

'Great riding, Morgan.' She could hear the other riders coming close as Morgan reined in. 'Didn't think you'd risk a valuable animal like Somali to save anyone's life. She must be really special ... don't we get an introduction?'

'Come on, little Red. Tell me what was so important to you that you had to risk your life and mine to get to me?'

Katriona's eyes flicked open to find his face only inches from her own, his grey eyes laughing down at her, wickedly teasing as if he knew that it was not only fear which was making her heart race in such an erratic fashion. Yet how could he know? She had just this minute discovered why she had followed him thousands of miles across the world. It was as if she had known what heaven it would be to be held close in his arms, to lean against his chest as if she belonged, to feel through the thin silk top the rapid beat of his heart.

As if reading a message in her eyes he gave a low exultant laugh and his lips claimed hers, sending the blood surging through her veins as he awakened an instant response deep within her, which would not be denied. As his firm mouth moved on hers, she felt as if she was being swept along on a glorious tide of emotion which would carry her off the edge of the world ...

'Didn't he do well?'

Appalled, Katriona heard the whistles and comments of the other riders and realised she had forgotten all about them. Too late, she knew, to retrieve that cool, prim and proper Miss Carmichael image. They had seen her arms automatically creep around Morgan's neck and her fingers bury themselves in his thick dark hair as she drew him ever closer to her, wanting the electricity flowing between them to weld them together for ever.

'Ross Carmichael's daughter!' Morgan's voice had a triumphant ring. 'Katriona, meet Jeff and Gary Travers, who are supposed to be working for your father, Phil and Rozanne Perry who are managing Hope Valley station across the river, and Wade and Ryan from the Lewis station. Meet Katriona Carmichael, folks.'

Katriona forced herself to smile as they acknowledged the introduction. She wished Morgan had left her to be trampled to death by the cattle; it would have been a lot less painful and embarrassing than meeting the disconcerting stare of this group. Whether they were amused by her behaviour or amazed by the fact that Ross had a daughter she could not tell. She wanted to hit Morgan Grant, to jump off his horse, but it seemed such a long way down.

'How did you get here, Katriona?' Morgan demanded.

'I came down that track behind the sheep yards. It was a bit rough ...'

'That would be the understatement of the year,' the tall blond Gary stated with an admiring laugh. 'You did well to get this far. It must have been mighty important.'

'I thought so at the time,' Katriona admitted with a husky laugh. 'I just wanted to say goodbye to Morgan. I'm sorry I messed up your work.'

Again it was Gary who spoke after the laughter died down. 'I congratulate you, Morgan. No girl ever got that desperate to kiss me goodbye. Perhaps if I practised that fancy riding bit ...'

'It wouldn't help you one bit,' his brother informed him unkindly. 'Come on, we'd better catch up with the cattle.'

Katriona was pleased to see them ride away. 'You can put me down now. I'll walk to the road.'

'That would be extremely foolish. We hope to drive the

cattle in that general direction and I don't want to risk Somali again.'

'Well, take your hands off me.' She tried to push his arm from her waist.

'Certainly.' He grinned and dropped his hand, touching Somali lightly with a spur. As the grey horse bounded forward Katriona's arms wrapped themselves convulsively around his neck and her slender body moulded itself against his. 'Blood and sand.'

With expert skill Morgan controlled the plunging horse, his sinewy suntanned arm snaking around her waist, bringing with it a feeling of complete security and sheer bliss. She pretended not to hear his triumphant shout of laughter as she snuggled closer to him when the horse changed its pace to a smooth, almost pleasurable rocking motion.

She felt his lips against her hair, against her ear. 'I'd have never reckoned you for a clinging vine, little Red.'

Katriona did not answer. For her, this moment was too precious to spoil with words.

CHAPTER FOUR

MORGAN reined Somali to a halt and lowered Katriona to the ground as they reached the edge of Horseshoe Lake.

'Are you there, Tim?'

Katriona saw a young man, standing by a jeep up on the edge of the main road, give Morgan an acknowledging wave.

'Good. I'm sending Katriona up to you. Give her my sweater to put on—it's in the jeep. We'll have one more try to get these cattle up before dark. See you . . . and you, Katriona.' Morgan galloped away.

That had been hours ago, thought Katriona wearily as she sat perched high on the stockyard's wide top rail. It had been exciting, watching the hard riding which had finally succeeded in bringing the wild cattle out on to the road and up past the homestead to these yards. It had been interesting listening to Tim explaining that they were not the well-bred station cattle of Evangeline but that they belonged to Hope Valley where the mustering was still done on horseback. It was wild rugged country and these cattle had successfully eluded being mustered for years, and now the new young manager and his wife were having a real clean-up. She had learned a lot from Tim, but was not sure she understood it all. These cattle were called cleanskins because they had never been mustered and earmarked so they did not legally belong to anyone. They had broken away from the musterers and ended up on Evangeline, and it was closer to their yards than back to Hope Valley yards.

That much Katriona could understand easily. What she could not understand was why they all stood talking there for hours after they had yarded the cattle. It was obvious to her that the musterers, the horses and the dogs were bone weary and exhausted. From snatches of conversation which came to her she gathered that they had been riding since before sun-up, yet here they were enjoying a good yarn as if they were not tired at all. The conversation wasn't even about the cattle ... not all the time. It was of the weather, sheep sales, rodeos, but mostly about people. She was slow to realise that these people were from three different stations, and that although their boundaries touched the station people rarely met up, and when they did they really enjoyed catching up on the news.

It was a beautifully clear evening and the moon hung low in the sky above the mountains; the sky was starting to be pinpricked with stars. Along the river wild ducks flew low, and then a flock of small birds swooped into a tree above the stockyards twittering noisily enough to be heard over the bellowing of the cattle. Katriona heard different birds calling and the roar of a stag in the park. Most birds and animals were quietly settling down for the night ... and she had no place to go. She sighed deeply. They belonged here, they had a right to stay in this beautiful place, while she had no right at all ... her mother had forfeited that right even before Katriona was born.

For a moment she was almost overwhelmed with bitterness. Angrily she pushed the painful thoughts from her. How stupid she was to want to stay here. Why, she had not known this beautiful valley existed until a few hours ago, so it was childish of her to have this deep-down feeling that she could be happy here. But the feeling persisted and grew as she looked down the long sweep of the station cradled in the nest of the mountains. It had a wildness, a lonely beauty which caught at her heart, and one with which she could easily identify, as if she had inside her a homing device which zeroed in on this one spot in the whole world which said she belonged.

It was stupid, crazy, yet she knew that no matter how far she travelled, all her life through would be haunted by the might-have-been. She might have been born here ... she might have been a small girl growing up on the isolated station ... she might have been a spoiled and petted daughter of that tough old man up at the homestead. She might have been given a pony and a dog and a room of her own—and the last, most painful might-have-been of all ... she might have been *loved*.

She shivered in spite of the glorious homespun warmth of Morgan's sweater. The darkness had fallen swiftly and the wind felt cold against her cheeks. She touched her face, surprised to find it wet with tears. Angrily she brushed them away. What a baby she was, crying for the moon! She hugged the sweater about her, revelling in the man's smell of it as much as its protection ... the Morgan smell of it.

'Are you going to stay up there all night?' Katriona became conscious of the fact that the crowd had gone and Morgan was standing below her. 'The boys have taken Somali for me, so I'll take you home in the truck. Can you get down by yourself?'

'Of course I can. What do you take me for?' she replied indignantly as she moved stiffly to get down from the rails.

'I take you for a very tired girl,' Morgan answered gently. 'Come along now.' He put out his hand to help her over the rough ground.

Katriona brushed his offer of help aside brusquely. 'Don't pretend concern for me. You pushed me into that study on my own today. You're a sadist!'

Morgan laughed. 'Hey, it wasn't that bad. You must have known it wouldn't be an easy meeting for either of you, and later on you'll be grateful to me for at least giving you some privacy.'

'I'll never be grateful to you, Morgan Grant!'

He held the truck door open for her. 'What you need is a hot bath, a good meal and a soft bed. Tomorrow things will look better.'

'Great little old philosopher, aren't you?' Katriona spat the words out furiously. 'You're right, though ... tomorrow I'll feel much better, because I won't be within shouting distance of Evangeline. I hope you're dog-tired and exhausted, and looking forward to your own hot bath, good meal and soft bed, because it will give me enormous satisfaction to keep you from them for a while. Your first job is to get my cases from the homestead, and the second is to drive me to a hotel in the nearest town . . .'

'Come now, you've got yourself all upset. You poor wee thing . . .'

'Don't you patronise me, you . . . you monster!' Katriona glared up at Morgan. 'I've got myself upset, have I? That's a laugh! You were the one who insisted I should come to this rotten place. You said my father wanted to see me. Well, you lied, Morgan Grant, you lied. Meeting me was the last thing he wanted to do. I know he's just as upset by this whole silly business as I am, and I hope the first thing he does when he sees you is to send you packing!'

Morgan roared with laughter. 'And you have the flaming nerve to accuse me of being a sadist! No hot bath, nothing to eat, no soft bed, and I get the sack on top of all that. You're a proper little spitfire when you're mad, aren't you, little Red?'

'And you can stop calling me Little Red!' Katriona would never forgive him for laughing. 'I'm glad the situation amuses you. Hurting people never appealed to my sense of humour.'

'For the small economy pack you carry a powerful punch, Katriona Carmichael. I don't think the situation is funny . . . just yourself. I think you've got hold of the wrong end of the stick, and you're trying to beat me to death with it. There's just no way that the boss would have been rude to you, or that he would have made you feel unwelcome. It's not in him to be rude to a lady, more's the pity.'

'You like men who are rude to ladies?'

'Only when the occasion demands it,' Morgan answered calmly. 'For instance, if you keep me standing here holding this door open for much longer you're going to get a prime sample of just how rude I can be. I've been very patient, I'm very tired . . . I'm covered in mud, and the wind is chilling me to the bone, so get in. *Now!*'

Katriona flinched nervously as he raised his voice on the last word, but her chin lifted defiantly. 'Not until you promise me that you'll take me to the nearest town straight away.'

Morgan reacted instantly; grabbing her by the shoulders he gave her a vigorous shake. 'Your first lesson—don't ever attempt to bargain with me. That goes for the first five minutes you're here or for the next fifty years if you stay. I don't trust women ... I don't bargain with women ... they're a poor lot at keeping bargains. Now, I'm going to get into this vehicle and drive home. If you want to travel with me, be seated by the time I get round my side of the truck. If you prefer to walk up there in the dark communing with nature or whatever, feel entirely free. I'm not forcing you either way.'

He shook her again and then let her go so abruptly that Katriona nearly fell. Oh, how she hated him! He was a great big bully ... and he was not bluffing. She could tell that he meant what he said and that if she did not get in quickly she would be left standing in the dark while he drove off. She climbed in and slammed the door as hard as she could. How could she have thought only such a short time ago that she could be happy on Evangeline? She must have been away with the fairies! No one could be happy with this arrogant brute throwing his weight around. She could not wait to get away.

Morgan maintained a stony silence all the way along to the house, which pleased Katriona. When they pulled up in the warm circle of light in front of the homestead, she tensed in her seat, her attractively fragile face set stubbornly.

Morgan sighed and ran his hand through his thick unruly hair. 'Are you always as contrary as this, Katriona Carmichael, or are you making a special effort just for me?'

'As contrary as what?' Katriona demanded mutinously.

'Ask a stupid question ...' Morgan thrummed the steering wheel with impatient fingers. 'Let me put it this way. I'm tired and I'm going inside to grab a shower, change and have my dinner. Now, I would feel a good deal more comfortable if you would join me ...'

'I don't shower with men I hardly know,' Katriona interjected flippantly.

'I'm trying very hard to be polite and reasonable, but something tells me time is running out. There's a limit to my control and you're pushing it. I would like you to accompany me inside, have a wash and a meal and we'll discuss the problem ...'

'Whose problem?'

'However,' Morgan continued smoothly as if she hadn't spoken, 'if you prefer to sit out here in splendid isolation until I'm ready, that's your choice.'

'It *is* my choice,' Katriona stated adamantly.

'So be it.' Morgan sounded tired as he unfolded his long length from the truck and walked up the path to the house, and disappeared without a backward glance.

Katriona felt quite alone, frustrated, cold, hungry and very, very mad. She was not wanted here, so she would not stay. She would not go back inside the homestead and be humiliated by Morgan or her father. Morgan Grant was *impossible*! Just because he was tall and good-looking he thought he could always get his own way. Well, she had news for him! Strange how their personalities clashed, each encounter ending up in a shower of sparks. Katriona had never wanted to scream and shout at any other man the way she did at Morgan. Perhaps she had never cared enough about winning out against any other man except Morgan. But she cared about Morgan Grant.

She felt the colour flare in her cold cheeks as she thought of the kiss he had given her after he had pulled her up in the saddle in front of him. It had just been a spontaneous reaction from him, a bit of a joke, but to her ... All the excitement of that moment came rushing back to her, the closeness and the warmth, and his eyes laughing down into hers, then the kiss, so short but unbelievably sweet. Katriona's lips curved in an enchanting reminiscent smile. Surely she would never regret coming here. A kiss like that, from a man like that, was worth flying to the moon and back to collect. Her blue eyes were dreamy.

The truck door jerked open. 'Glad you've found something about Evangeline to make you smile.' Her father stood there with a suitcase and overcoat in his hand. 'The way Morgan ripped into me, I thought I was being tried for cruel and inhuman practices. Actually I think you scored more hits than I did.'

Katriona bit her lip in silence.

Her father gave her a rueful smile. 'You don't agree? Very well, you must deserve an apology, Miss Carmichael. If I've given any offence I hope you'll forgive me, it was not intentional.'

Katriona choked on a lump in her throat. It was not right to have this proud hawk-like old man apologising to her. 'Please don't. I shouldn't have come here to embarrass you. It was my mistake, not yours. My rudeness, not yours.'

Her father put down his case and overcoat and leaned against the open door of the truck. 'I've not got a lot of time. I'm driving through to Christchurch to catch a late plane to Auckland. I've cut it a bit fine already, but I simply can't leave until you and I have this thing straightened out between us. I'll be away at least a week. While I'm away I would like you to stay on the station and get to know it a little—get the feel of the place. I wish I didn't have to go at this time, but this conference is most important for my business. It was arranged months ago, so I'll have to postpone the pleasure of getting to know you for just a little while.'

His tone was sincere and his smile was warm. This old warrior had charm, Katriona thought. 'Thank you for your invitation ... your very kind invitation, but I think it's better that I leave. I'm not angry or upset. As I said this afternoon, I did want to meet you, and I'm pleased that I came. I really feel that I mustn't trespass on your hospitality further.'

For a split second she saw fire flash in his eyes, almost like the light of battle. This man did not expect to be refused ... anything. 'So you've decided not to forgive me. Morgan was correct! I must have hurt you very much. I'm truly saddened by your decision.'

'No, it's nothing like that,' Katriona protested. 'Really I quite understand that my sudden appearance must have been quite a shock for you. I should have let you know I was arriving. I do apologise if I've caused you any pain or embarrassment.' It sounded so stilted and formal, yet funnily enough she meant every word of it.

'You're causing me considerable embarrassment right now, young lady. You're my daughter, my only daughter, and one short half-hour visit with me is enough to convince you that you're better off without me than with me. I'm truly humiliated. It took your mother a little longer to conclude that I was entirely useless as a husband, so I can only surmise that you're much more intelligent than she was, because it took you such a short time to form your irrevocable decision. History repeating itself, will be the way the district describes it.'

Katriona was appalled. Her father seemed to shrink before her eyes, his voice became faded and old, his hand held over his face, shielding his emotion from her eyes, was shaking a little. How selfish she was! Always thinking of herself, of her own independent nature. She had not given her father a thought. He had to go on living here. And she had not had the insight to know that he would naturally couple her behaviour with her mother's.

'Please—it's not like that at all. If it's all that important to you ...'

'You'll stay? I have your word on that?' His voice was muffled and his face still concealed.

'Yes. Yes, I'll stay until you get back,' Katriona conceded.

'But then I won't get time to talk with you. Make it a month. You're young, a month out your life is not too much to ask for, surely? Be generous to an old man.' His hand lowered, shrewd blue eyes met Katriona's demanding a favourable answer.

Defeated, she sighed, 'I'll stay a month.' It was against her better judgment, but she felt incredibly guilty, even though she could not fathom the reason.

Her father straightened up abruptly. 'Glad that's settled. I'll take you inside, then I'll be on my way.'

Katriona was outraged. Gone was the tired old man image and back was the confident and eminently capable man she had met in the study earlier. She shot out of the truck and accused him, 'Mr Carmichael, you're a shocking fraud! You don't give a damn if I stay or not. You don't give a damn what the district says about you. You're not honest ...'

'Now, now ... Morgan said you had a hasty temper.' He smiled at her benevolently and half raised his hand to silence her protest. 'My motives were honest, I did want you to agree to stay, but my methods may not have been ... strictly correct. So you see, to get you to stay I had to appeal to your better nature. Don't you think it's worth something to know that I believe you had a better nature?'

'But why? Why did you want me to stay?' Katriona demanded.

'Because Morgan said I couldn't get you to change your mind. I rely on his judgment quite a lot, but every now and again I need to prove him wrong ... for his own sake, of course. It stops him getting bigheaded, you know.' He looked at her quizzically with an impish light in his eyes.

For a moment Katriona held her anger against him, then she laughed, unable to help herself. 'It doesn't stop him from being arrogant and over-sure of himself, but I don't blame you for trying. I think you're a wicked old man, Mr Carmichael, but I'll forgive you. If you'd been honest and said you wanted to cut Morgan Grant down to size, I would have been quite willing to go along with you. It would have saved you all that over-acting.'

He dropped his arm lightly on her shoulders. 'Mr Carmichael is too formal. Most folk call me Ross and I'd be most pleased if you would too, Katriona. I think you and I could get along most agreeably. Let's go and face up to Morgan. It will do me good to see his face. And thank you for agreeing to stay.'

They looked up as her father piloted her through the door. 'Morgan, I'd be grateful if you'd take good care of my daughter Katriona while I'm up North. I'll leave her in your hands and I'll hold you accountable.'

He gave them a nonchalant wave, flicked Katriona's cheek gently. 'Evangeline is worth knowing, Katriona. Go to it ... Morgan could be the key.' The words were for her alone, and he left before she could answer.

'It will be a pleasure to look after you, Katriona. Follow me. It's okay, Nivvy, you finish your meal.'

'Thank you,' muttered Katriona as he held the door open for her. She felt a bit bemused. Too much drama ... and she felt foolish in Morgan's thick sweater ... it dwarfed her completely.

'Your bedroom, and the bathroom is directly opposite. There's your case. Take your time, Nivvy has your meal in the oven.' Morgan reached the door and then swung round. 'The cunning old eagle! How did he do it? How did he make you change your mind? I told him he'd not get you out of that truck without using gelignite ... the high explosive stuff.'

'Perhaps that's what he used,' Katriona parried.

'No, he's got a more subtle touch than that. You're not telling?'

Katriona shook her head emphatically. That was a secret she would keep, a secret she shared with her father. Her eyes were very bright and full of devilment. 'Perhaps when you're as old as Ross you'll have as much charm and skill as he has at his command.'

'Fallen for the old eagle, have you?' Morgan grinned then left the room.

Conscious that she had already caused enough delay, Katriona showered quickly, and chose a froth of a dress from her case, made of muslin with lace and ribbon insertions. She brushed her hair and caught it back with a pale green scarf which matched the ribbon on her dress, touched her face with the barest minimum of make-up, lipstick and eye-shadow, and hesitated in front of the mirror. She looked so *young* in this outfit, but she had chosen it in deliberate contrast to the heavy-knit knee-length sweater of her last appearance. She strapped on her elegant high-heeled shoes, delighted with the extra inches they gave her.

As she paused in the doorway Morgan came forward with a look of warm approval on his face. 'I'm glad you decided to stay.'

The words were trite, but his laughter-lit grey eyes were transmitting all sorts of incredible messages to Katriona and she was aware that she was blushing like an idiot. What a give-away! A starry-eyed teenager with a crush on a pop star would probably have the same infatuated grin on her face. It was not fair. After years of being completely im-mune to all masculine charm and appeal she was being utterly devastated by Morgan Grant. And, what was worse, she was sure that he knew exactly the effect that he was having on her, that the electricity between them was melt-ing her very bones.

Determinedly she tore her gaze from his. 'I'm starving!'

'I can see that,' he laughed mockingly, pretending to mis-understand. 'Oh, you mean for food.'

Katriona blushed so deeply that she was sure the colour must spread right down her bare neck and shoulders. She followed him to the table where Mrs Niven and two young men were sitting drinking coffee.

'Ah, thanks, Nivvy, you've put Katriona beside me. I don't know if you've all been properly introduced, but this is Katriona, Ross's daughter, as you'll have guessed. Kat-riona, this is Mrs Niven, and these two you met by Horse-shoe Lake this afternoon, Gary and Jeff Travers.'

Mrs Niven acknowledged the introduction with a smile. 'We met this afternoon too.' She placed a plate in front of Katriona. 'I hope your meal hasn't spoiled. I didn't know Ross had a daughter, but it's lovely to have you here for a visit.'

Both men were on their feet waiting to shake her hand. They were obviously brothers, tall, slimly built and blond, with American accents. Jeff smiled as he took her hand. 'A real pleasure.'

Gary gave her a cheeky grin. 'Howdy! You could say there's a real family likeness, but thank God you're a lot prettier than Ross.' Still holding her hand lightly, he turned to Morgan. 'She's as light as thistledown. No wonder you could do your spectacular rescue stunt with just a flick of your wrist. Why, if there was a good draught she'd float away on gossamer wings ...'

'She might yet, if you don't let her sit down and have her meal,' Morgan said a little roughly.

Katriona enjoyed her dinner of well cooked roast beef and rich gravy and vegetables. It was friendly and companionable to have them all linger on over their coffee while she ate her meal, and listened to their farm talk. Not that she understood much of it, but if she was to be here for a month she might not be such a dummy. When she had finished her steamed pudding with rich yellow sauce and whipped cream she helped Mrs Niven clear the table and stack the dishes in the automatic dishwasher, in spite of the housekeeper's protest that she should go and join the men folk in the lounge.

Katriona laughed, 'We both will, when we've tidied up. That was a beautiful meal, but I need some exercise now.'

They took more coffee with them when they finally went through to the large comfortable lounge which had a cheerful fire burning in a magnificent stone fireplace. Only moments later there came the sound of a car being driven fast roaring up the steep bluff and squealing to a halt.

'Carla,' Morgan announced, getting to his feet. 'I'll get another cup for her.'

'Boy, is she in for a shock!' Gary commented with a significant look in Mrs Niven's direction. There was a great deal of satisfaction in his voice.

Katriona clutched her cup of coffee, nervously wondering who Carla was. It was quite obvious that Gary meant that she was the shock. She did not have to wait long. Carla swept into the room like a tornado. She was a striking-looking girl, tall, blonde and curvy, wearing a green suit with all the flair of a top fashion model, her face superbly made up, her brilliant brown eyes highlighted by the scarf so casually knotted at her throat.

She dropped her leather bag and gloves on the coffee table and walked to the fire with outstretched hands. 'Oh, I adore a fire! If I'd been born in the Stone Age I'd have made a fabulous fire-worshipper.' She struck a dramatic pose as Morgan came through with the coffee. 'How would I do as a fire goddess, Morgan darling?'

'A fire devil would suit your character better,' Morgan smiled indulgently at her exquisite face. 'Coffee?'

'For me? You really are sweet, Morgan, you must be rewarded.' She leaned forward and kissed him on the cheek.

'Lucky Morgan,' commented Gary wickedly. 'Two beautiful women bestowing kisses on him in one day. How do you do it, mate?'

Katriona could have murdered him as she felt the blush stain her cheeks.

'And who was the other one?' Carla's voice had all the sharpness of a diamond saw.

'Ross's daughter, Katriona Carmichael. Come and meet her, Carla.' Morgan's expression was enigmatic.

Carla turned as Katriona stood up. Shock and disbelief were written on her face.

Gary took Katriona's cup from her, saying maliciously, 'Now, Katriona, don't be upset. I know your kiss was different . . . Morgan kissed you, whereas Carla kissed Morgan, technically speaking.'

'Shut up!' Carla, white-faced with anger, pushed Gary aside. 'Rubbish, absolute rubbish. Ross never had any children.'

'Ross accepts Katriona as his daughter, and Katriona accepts Ross as her father, so you'll have to bow to the inevitable, Carla.' Morgan was quite firm.

'I'll not accept her. Where's Ross?' Carla demanded, her voice like a whiplash.

'In Christchurch, flying North for a week. His last order

was for me to look after his daughter. Katriona, I would like you to meet Carla Grayson, Ross's niece.'

Carla stormed forward. 'Where did you spring from? Why haven't we heard of you before now?'

Katriona eyed her steadily. 'I haven't heard of you before either, but I believe you're Ross's niece.'

'Don't you come smart with me, girl! You may have fooled this lot, but you'll have to work a lot harder to convince me. When did you arrive?'

'This afternoon,' Katriona answered with studied care, hoping the other girl would not sense how nervous she was.

'Good God! You calmly walk in here and announce that you're Ross's daughter and he falls on your neck. You've got *nerve*!' Carla's tone was venomous.

'I hope so.'

Morgan spoke sharply. 'That will do, Carla. We're not stupid. I met Katriona when I was in Scotland last year.'

Carla exploded. 'You ... you miserable creep! So you're behind it all. You've been sitting on this ... gloating over it, for a year, have you? Well, you won't get away with it, I can promise you that. I'm off to see Ross. I know what you're up to, but it won't work. Of all the devious, underhand, contemptible ... And you, whatever your name is, don't get too comfortable in your new role. It won't be long before you're on your way back from wherever they dug you out from!'

Carla snatched up her bag and whirled out of the room. Seconds later they heard the motor of her car spring to life, then saw the flash of headlights as she turned and drove past the house, then silence.

'Aw! She didn't drink her coffee,' said Gary with mock concern.

Katriona felt quite sick and shaken, her face was pale and her blue eyes wide with shock. It had been an incredible scene, especially in that friendly relaxed atmosphere.

'Your comments didn't help the situation, Gary.' Morgan sounded slightly ruffled. He touched Katriona sympathetically on the shoulder. 'Sorry about that, Katriona, it was inexcusable, but Carla lives on her nerves.'

Mrs Niven stood up and stated vigorously, 'You're wrong, Morgan. Carla lives on everyone else's nerves, and mine more than most. You'll have to excuse me, I'm off to bed. And please, Katriona, don't feel troubled by Carla, each of us here has felt the rough edge of her tongue, Jeff, Gary, and myself ... and when she's feeling lucky, Morgan.'

The warm understanding smile Mrs Niven gave Katriona eased a little the tightness in her chest. 'I'll go with you. I've had a long day too.'

'But I wanted to have a bit of a talk with you,' Morgan protested. 'There's a few things I'd like to explain.'

'They'll keep.' Katriona replied wearily. 'You could have warned me, but you didn't. Goodnight.' She followed Mrs Niven to the door before she remembered the boys. 'Goodnight, Jeff, Gary.'

They were on their feet instantly. 'Goodnight.' Then Gary spoke again. 'We're glad you came. We'll see you enjoy yourself.'

'They're nice boys,' Mrs Niven commented. 'Like most of the Americans we get here they have lovely manners.'

'Do you get many?' Katriona asked, not really caring.

'Quite a few. A sort of feedback from when Morgan went over to the States as a Field scholar.'

'I'll say goodnight, Mrs Niven, and thanks for your kindness,' said Katriona as she reached her door. She did not want any further talk. There had been too many words already today.

CHAPTER FIVE

It was still dark when Katriona woke next morning, and she lay quietly trying to orientate herself. A wave of exhilaration swept over her as she remembered she was at Evangeline, her father's station—all sixty-three thousand acres of it, with mountains, lakes, rivers and streams. She pressed her digital watch and saw the time was only five-fifteen. She slipped from her bed and in the half light pulled on her shirt and bib-styled overalls, her fingers fumbling and shaking as she clipped the huge shiny clasps. She shivered, not knowing whether it was from cold or excitement. She added a heavy Scottish sweater and slipped her feet into rope sandals, then crept outside hoping not to wake anyone.

Once in the yard she could see the lights on in the woolshed and made her way towards them, climbing once more over the padlocked gate. Ahead of her was another gate under the tall dark plantations and although she longed to explore she was a little afraid of getting lost. She would wait until daylight. Through the fence in front of the woolshed were sheep grazing by a small building. It was painted green with a white door and it beckoned. The sheep scattered in alarm as she made her way to the step and sat down hugging her knees. She smiled as the sheep inched forward to peer at her curiously for a few minutes before making up their minds that she was entirely harmless, and they resumed their original positions in a semi-circle near her, nonchalantly chewing.

Her eyes lifted to the twin peaks of the mountain across the river. She could not see the Hope River, just the sheer bluff walls above it, but she knew it was there, that liquid silver ribbon winding its way through the gorge. Native bush ran in tongues down the gullies by it and higher up

95

were the plateaux which gave away again to more bush and shingle slides, and right near the peak of the hill was a fan-shaped crater. To her delight she saw one pale star pinning the early dawn sky above the twin peaks.

Then came the plaintive haunting cry of the kea. She had heard it last evening when Tim had stopped by the cage on his way to the stockyards. He said it called each morning at dawn and in the late evening. Suddenly a flock of sparrows flew over her head, like a squadron of tiny jets dark against the yellow brown mountains. Katriona followed their flight until they disappeared behind the trees by the silo. Then as if they were only pathfinders, flock after flock followed, some of twenties, some of hundreds. Well, they seemed to know where they were going and she envied them.

Slowly she looked around her nearer to hand. There was the huge woolshed with the light streaming through the windows. It had stained dark brown wooden walls, with a green-painted roof and the window sashes neatly outlined in white. She could just see the top of another station roof painted green, with the white vee of the eaves showing and a white chimney to the right of the woolshed. Who lived there? She wanted to meet them, to know what work they did on the station, how long they'd lived here and did they love it too?

The sheep yards were empty, neat, well kept and functional, as was everything she had seen on Evangeline—all spoke of care, good planning and excellent management. That meant thinking of Morgan. And that was bad, because she had resolved not to think of Morgan, and more especially not to think of Morgan and Carla . . . She would blank him right out of her mind and concentrate on getting to know Evangeline. That was what her father had told her to do. Certainly he had said Morgan could be the key . . . but he did not have to be the only key.

Her father! It was true that she had got over the surprise that she actually did have a father, but he had just been a nebulous figure in her mind until yesterday afternoon.

What a man! There was a power in him, strength of character, and integrity—yes, she could feel all these. She did not doubt that he could be hard, even cruel, but the sudden change to humour and charm had really surprised her. A man used to getting his own way always, ruthless, maybe ... Morgan was like that too ...

Damn Morgan Grant! There he was getting in the road of her thought patterns again. But he was like her father in some ways, a younger version, but just as hard, just as steel-like and determined. She knew that was the truth. She just had one month to get to know them, these two men who had made such a vivid impression on her. Her pulses raced at the prospect of the mental stimulation involved in trying to discover what made them what they were. It would be a real challenge indeed, because she could feel in each of them a depth which would be hard to fathom. They would keep their inner selves hidden from her, she had no doubt. She would do her best to learn about them, and then she would leave, never to return.

Thirty days only, not long, but it had to last her a lifetime. She must not stay longer, not one day longer than that, or it would prove her undoing. She shivered. Morgan Grant must never know why she had travelled so far. to see him. He must always believe she only wanted to meet her father. He must always believe that she was going back to Tiree to marry Donald. She was only safe as long as he thought that ... safe, a strange word to set her heart pounding the way it had last night when he held her in his arms.

'It that all you've got to do? You'll never learn about the station sitting dreaming and watching the sun come up.'

Katriona jumped nervously as she recognised Morgan's voice. She felt the colour stain her cheeks. 'My father said to get the feel of the place, and that's what I was doing until you came along and disturbed me.'

'Oh, I'm sorry I disturb you, Katriona,' he mocked lightly.

'You do *not* disturb me,' Katriona replied furiously. 'You

disturb the peace and quiet of the morning, that's what I meant.'

Her bright blue eyes flashed sparks as she looked up at him, only to flicker away from the lean masculine face with the teasing grey eyes which seemed to read her every thought. Dear God, was she so transparent! She bit her bottom lip hard as she bent her head, pretending to adjust her sandal, and heard him chuckle.

A sharp whistle made her look across at the iron gate, where a shepherd sat for a moment with his four dogs below him, then he dropped to the ground and walked over to open the yard gate while one dog snaked around the sheep by the cottage. Katriona listened and watched entranced as he worked his dog with a series of whistles. She heard him call, 'Wayleggo Fan', and his dog came to heel, then he sent another two out and seconds later all the sheep were penned.

As she looked back to the gate she saw a large red truck being driven through it and backed up to the woolshed. A man appeared high up in a loft doorway shouting, 'Clear that barley off the deck', and seconds later started heaving down sheepskins to the young man below.

Then a large modern car swung through the gateway and round the front of the truck and pulled up by the yards, and half a dozen athletic-looking men climbed out, laughing and talking. Suddenly there was noise and movement everywhere, and Katriona felt her eyes weren't big enough to hold it all.

'The shearers arriving to do the crutching,' Morgan said quietly.

Katriona glanced up in surprise to find him still standing there. She had forgotten him completely. He was not smiling now, just watching her intently, his whole attention riveted on her reactions, yet from the top of his dark head to the soles of his boots he appeared relaxed. It was only then that she became aware that he was stripped to the waist like the shearers. He wore only grey shorts and heavy woollen socks and boots, and the sun shone a golden glow on his deeply tanned body highlighting the broad sinewy torso, the tapering hips and long muscular legs, giving him the likeness of an athlete sculptured in bronze, a perfect study.

'I've missed the sunrise,' Katriona cried.

'There'll be other mornings.' He spoke sympathetically as if he understood her loss.

'Twenty-nine.' Katriona met his gaze now. Her blue eyes were steady and direct, free from embarrassment. 'Only twenty-nine.' She turned to the east where the sun struck bright in a blue blue sky, silhouetting the line of tall slender poplars and turning golden the tussock-clad hills.

'Why?' Morgan's tone was sharp, demanding an answer.

'I must leave at the end of the month.'

'Donald's orders?' Sarcasm was heavy in his voice.

'My own,' Katriona replied tersely. They had been so close, just for a second, and now she was angry and resentful again. He seemed to be able to play on her moods as an expert violinist plays on a Stradivarius.

A truck stopped by the gate near the pines and a man hopped down to hold it open. They drove through, followed by someone on a motor-bike, then another motor-bike with a cage trailer holding dogs. They all waved and Katriona and Morgan waved back. Another van and another motor-bike went through before the gate was closed.

'Where are they all going? Do they all work here?' Katriona asked.

'Yes, they all work here. They're going up the lane which runs through the farm. The first were the fencing contractors who are heading up on the hill to fence the new deer block, the second lot were a shepherd with his dogs going for more sheep, then the head tractor driver and the last one another tractor driver.'

'Haven't they got any names?' Katriona demanded indignantly.

'Oh, yes, little Red, they've all got names, and you can talk with them and find out who they are, what their work is, and each piece of information you gather will help you learn about your father's station, and about him, because his station is his heart and his heart is Evangeline.'

'And your heart, where is it?' Katriona was appalled to hear herself ask.

Morgan laughed. 'You do want all the answers, Katriona Carmichael, but that's one you'll have to work out for yourself. It will take you a while, believe me.'

Katriona was furious with herself, shocked that she could have been so stupid. So much for subtlety! 'It really doesn't interest me all that much,' she remarked in what she hoped was a detached manner.

'My, what big blue eyes you have!' Morgan was taunting her again. 'Do you know that the eyes are the windows of the soul?'

Immediately her long dark lashes fanned her cheeks, but she could not control the blush which dyed her cheeks. She could have cheerfully murdered him. If only she had not restricted her private life so drastically she might have been practised in hiding her emotions, instead of feeling completely naked. She would hopefully improve as the days went on, but at this very moment she wanted to put some distance between herself and Morgan. It was vital he did not discover her susceptibility to him.

'Morning, Morgan.'

'Morning, Tay. Come and meet Katriona Carmichael, Ross's daughter. I presume the news had already reached you? Katriona, this is Taylor Young, Head Shepherd of Evangeline.'

Katriona had been so preoccupied with her own thoughts that she had not heard the truck drive up. She stood up, and found herself dwarfed between the two men, both well over six foot. 'It's a pleasure to meet you, Mr Young.'

'It's a great pleasure to meet you, Miss Carmichael. By the way, Tay will do just fine.' He put his hand out.

'And my name is Katriona,' she responded as she took his hand. She could really like this fair-haired giant with his warm easy smile and deep brown eyes.

'Tay, you're more fortunate than I was with my first

meeting with Katriona. I don't seem to recall you saying it was a pleasure to meet me ...'

'I didn't, and it wasn't,' Katriona glared at him.

'Gave you a hard time, did he, Katriona?' Tay looked sympathetic. 'He can be pretty mean to handle.'

'He was,' Katriona agreed wholeheartedly.

Tay gave Morgan a lazy grin. 'I hear via the cookhouse that you fared better at a subsequent meeting. That should console you.'

Morgan smiled at Katriona with mischief in his eyes. 'Oh, I think it would be fair to say our relationship is improving rapidly.'

'It is not! You took an unfair advantage ...'

Morgan shouted with laughter. 'An unfair advantage of the situation. Did I ever! What man wouldn't?'

'A gentleman,' Katriona retorted.

'Chalk that one up to you, Katriona,' Tay commented. 'From what I hear you must have been doing okay yesterday in many ways. The gorgeous Carla as well!'

Something in Tay's voice made Katriona glance hastily at Morgan. His smile had disappeared and his eyes were chill and cold. 'I should mention that Katriona is here for only one month. Ross wants her to learn as much as possible about Evangeline in that time.'

'Tall order for a small girl,' Tay smiled down at Katriona. 'I'll be happy to help you any way that I can. Starting from now if you like. I'm just going up to the clover paddock for a mob of ewes. I'll talk to you on the way.'

Katriona did not need a second invitation. There was something strange going on between these two men, and she wanted out. Even before Tay had arrived she had been needing some respite from Morgan's perceptive eyes. As she climbed into the truck and slammed the door, Tay took his place beside her, and she saw Morgan move as if he was going to protest her decision. Then he changed his mind as they drove off and gave them a wave before striding towards the woolshed.

'You can chalk that one up to me,' Tay said cheerfully,

giving Katriona a wink as he circled round through the iron gate and turned towards the plantation. He stopped in front of the gate.

Katriona sat and looked at him questioningly.

'The passenger always opens and shuts the gate,' Tay told her quietly.

'Sorry.' Katriona half jumped, half fell from the truck in her anxiety to get the gate open. She could just imagine Morgan's sarcasm if he had been driving. As the truck drove through she saw about six dog crates were on the deck. Evangeline was really fully mechanised, even the dogs did not have to walk. She saw Morgan watching her from beside the woolshed, and she knew he was angry, although she did not know why. She gave him a cheeky wave as she ran for the truck and climbed in without looking back.

As the truck climbed the hill Katriona looked about her with delight. 'It's so beautiful here. Do you know the names of the trees?'

'The big one by the gate is a sequoia, a Canadian redwood; there are ash and elm, wild cherry, wild plum, and of course the Scotch firs of the plantation. They were planted by the original owner of Evangeline, a Frenchman, Count de la Pasteur, way back in 1864. Sounds a romantic start for a good old New Zealand station, don't you think, Katriona?'

'Yes, yes, it does. I like the idea.'

'You do like a little romance in your life, Katriona?'

'If you're getting at me about that kiss Morgan gave me, you can forget it!' Katriona flared, then stopped and looked at Tay and smiled. He had not been teasing her. He was just interested in her reply, and his brown eyes were kind. 'Sorry,' she offered swiftly.

'I'm sorry too,' Tay grinned lazily at her. 'I should have realised that any girl who's spent an hour with Morgan straight after breakfast . . .'

'I didn't have any breakfast,' Katriona giggled ruefully.

'Oh, it would be much worse on an empty stomach . . .

where was I? Oh yes, a girl would definitely be on the defensive, and slightly hair-triggered ...'

'What's hair-triggered?'

'Umm! Finely tuned temper-wise, if I could put it nicely, or ready to shoot at the slightest provocation. And you do have red hair.'

Katriona laughed. 'That's something I can't deny.'

Tay laughed with her. 'You and I are going to be friends, I can feel it in my bones.'

'So do I. Oh, look down there!' Katriona squirmed around to look out of the back window of the truck. 'From here I can see the woolshed and yards, and the homestead, the cookhouse and men's quarters, and the deer in the park, and a house ... your house, Tay?'

'You're not doing badly—yes, that's my house. And talking of romance, I think I've almost cornered the market as far as love and romance go on Evangeline. You'll have to meet my wife and kids, then you'll know what I mean. They'll love you.'

'If they do, I'll just love them right back, and you too.' Was she going crazy? Saying things like that to a man she hardly knew? Why, he could take it any number of ways. She looked across at Tay nervously and then relaxed as she met his pleasant smile. She pulled her thick sweater off, hoping that a little action might cool the sudden swinging happiness that threatened to make a shambles out of her regulated and confined emotions. She drew a deep breath, but it was no use. It must be the high country air, intoxicating, heady like wine, which was making her say things completely out of character. She felt the air beautiful about her, and the fantastic heat of the morning sun streaming through the window was making her expand and grow like a hothouse plant, making her throw caution to the wind and say what she really felt. After a lifetime of being restrained and regimented and cautious, it was exhilarating to be completely natural with someone—a fabulous, unexpected luxury.

'May I go out with you a lot? You could teach me so

much. Morgan treats me as if I'm intellectually handicapped. Oh, look down there, Tay, a tiny wee lake ... oh, it's perfect, just perfect! I just love it here.'

'I can see that. And yes to your other question, you can come with me whenever you like.' He stopped in front of a gate and Katriona did not have to be told twice. She was out of the truck in an instant, swinging the gate wide open. 'Hop in. We'll bring the sheep back this way so we'll leave it open.' He waved to a man on a tractor. 'That's Phil, the second tractor driver. You would see him go by on the bike this morning.'

'Yes, I did. What's he doing? Where does he live?'

'He's giant discing the barley stubble, working it up, then it will lie fallow for the winter before being planted again in the early spring. He's a single man, so lives in the men's quarters and takes his meals at the cookhouse.'

Katriona watched the golden stubble change to the rich dark soil colour as the tractor passed, and they drove on through the next paddock. Suddenly the tremendous sweep of the land overwhelmed her, the immensity of the station, the grassed pasture lands, the tussock hills and the mountains simply seemed too much for her to comprehend. She would never learn about it in a week, a month or a lifetime. But she must try.

'Your wife won't mind me?'

'Amber? No, she won't mind. She'll encourage you, she loves this place as much as I do.'

'I've never met anyone named Amber,' said Katriona.

Tay agreed. 'Her mother had a most peculiar sense of humour, but somehow it suits her. Wait till you meet her, you'll know instantly that she couldn't be anything else but Amber.'

'You sound like a very lucky man,' Katriona said with a smile.

'Don't I know it! And she tells me every day just in case I should forget.'

A shadow chased across Katriona's attractive face as she thought of the messed-up marriages and the unhappiness her mother had caused. She asked a trifle anxiously, 'Are you ever likely to forget?'

As if sensing her mood and her need for an honest answer he replied seriously, 'Never. When you meet her you'll know what I mean; green eyes, black hair, beautiful, crazy, five foot nothing, a child one moment and all woman the next, a real power pack, and I love her very much. I'm a one-woman man.'

'She's a very lucky woman.' Katriona's voice was husky as she fought back the threatening tears. What was *wrong* with her? She was not an emotional person, rarely resorted to tears, and yet here she was ready to weep bucketsful of tears because this tall fair mountain man had declared his love for his wife so openly. This Evangeline must be getting to her. Perhaps she was suffering from jet-lag; it had to be something.

They were travelling through a paddock of yellow stubble where sheep were feeding when a flock of geese flew up and winged their way past the truck.

'Wild geese?'

'No. Domesticated. Although there are a flock of Canadian geese about.'

'But they fly like wild geese.' Katriona's voice was incredulous. 'Domesticated, away up here, miles from the homestead.'

'They sort of range free. You're not far from home in a direct line. You'll meet them up here, down by the lake, in the deer park. They go where they please. Even the pet pig, a Captain Cooker, visits each house to get the choice bits, but as he wanders down on the main road sometimes we had to paint the word PET on his side in case someone shot him thinking he was a wild pig.' Tay grinned as he went round to release a small alert brown dog from its crate.

Katriona watched it make a sweeping run across the field and disappear behind a hill. She thought dreamily that to range free in this wild lonely land would be all she'd ever ask for. To feel the wind in her hair, the hot sun on her face, to go where she pleased, and to be part of this beauty, to belong here for ever in these sunlight mountains would be heaven indeed. Was that why she was so emotional, so vibrant with feeling? Because there was no place for her here, no one to love her as Amber was loved. She knew that she was a one-man woman and knew just as surely that Morgan Grant was that man. How he would laugh if he knew!

She forced herself to take an interest in what Tay was doing and became intrigued with the cleverness of the small foxlike dog away up on the hillside bringing the sheep down to the flat. Implicitly it followed Tay's whistled commands, even though it rarely saw the sheep, and soon had the paddock mustered. Also gathered up were some very portly turkeys who had been feeding on the barley, and they were indignant as they hoisted their fat bodies up on the fence, gobbling in protest at their interrupted breakfast. 'Wayleggo, Maid! Wayleggo!'

Katriona heard again that unusual command and watched Maid come racing to heel. Tay let two more dogs go.

'Can you do all that? Work several dogs at a time just by whistling them?' Katriona asked.

'You can if you're a shepherd. In fact you have to if you're a shepherd. Some are good, some are bad. If there are any dog trials on while you're here we'll take you along, then you can see what the best in the country are like.'

'Can Morgan do it?'

'He's good, real good, and he's got some great dogs.'

'He would be,' Katriona retorted a little bitterly. 'I suppose he does everything well.'

'I wouldn't say that,' Tay replied with a grin. 'He hasn't made much of a job of charming the boss's daughter.'

'You're very young to be a head shepherd,' Katriona hurried to change the subject.

'Twenty-eight. A year older than Morgan. How old would you like me to be? Fifty?' He gave her a slow lazy smile. 'You've got to be young in this game, and fit, to walk the tops.' He waved his hand in the direction of the mountains.

'What are the tops?' Katriona demanded.

'The tops of the hills.'

'They're not hills, they're mountains,' she protested.

'Hills to me, mountains to you, same difference. I'll take you up there one day, that'll be a real experience for you ... that's unless Morgan objects.'

'Why should Morgan object?'

'Why should he indeed? Just a gut feeling I have,' Tay smiled at her. 'Tell him I'm taking you to the tops, I think his reaction might surprise you.'

'Nothing he does would surprise me,' Katriona snorted.

'I wouldn't bet on that one, Katriona.' Tay's grin was even broader. 'Let's get these old dears back to the yards.'

'Are you and Morgan good friends?' she asked, unable to contain her curiosity.

'Closer than blood brothers ... most of the time, but we do have the odd disagreement.' He was smiling broadly at some secret thought which he was obviously not going to share with Katriona.

It puzzled her for a few minutes, then she gave it away and sat quietly drinking in the beauty of the morning, and luxuriating in the heat of the sun. As she climbed back in the truck after shutting the gate she asked, 'Is all the land I can see Evangeline? Are all the fields named?'

'It's all Evangeline except the hills across the river. They're on the Hope Valley Station. Yes, for convenience, most paddocks are named. From here, Clover Paddock, Racecourse, Grandstand, over there Round Hill, Mount Skiddaw, Top Organs.'

Katriona followed his pointing hand, which dropped swiftly to bang on the truck door making the sheep move a bit faster to catch the main mob. 'I'll never learn all their names,' she wailed. 'I suppose this is only a tiny part of it.'

'You're correct there, but it's not all divided up with fencing as well as this place. See; there's Summerdale ... it was once a station on its own: nineteen thousand acres ...'

Tay stopped talking as he caught up on some stragglers and braked the truck. He leapt down from the seat and in a flash had grabbed two miserable-looking sheep up and deposited them in the empty dog crates, and rejoined her. 'See, that's where modern mechanisation has it all over the musterer on horseback. We'll pick up quite a few on the way down and they'll ride in style, whereas years ago they would have slowed up the whole drive.'

'I'd rather have horses than trucks and jeeps and motorbikes. There's no romance in . . .'

'Don't you dare say that,' Tay interrupted. 'Wait till you've been here a while and you'll find romance in watching a dozer inching its way up a mountainside, punching in roads where no roads went before, in trucks carrying men to the distant blocks at the back of the station, in bringing them home to their own beds each night instead of camping out for weeks at a time, in planes swooping in to topdress and spread fertiliser, and helicopters lifting and loading materials on these high country runs in a matter of minutes, saving men days of backbreaking toil and sweat. Oh, yes, Katriona, there's still romance here even if the horse has gone, new ideas, progress and expansion on a scale only dreamed of in previous years. The potential is unlimited on Evangeline.'

'Do Morgan and my father feel the same way as you do, Tay?' Katriona felt caught up in the enthusiasm in his voice.

Tay laughed. 'If you multiply what I feel by a thousand you might get close to what those two feel. High country stations demand their own kind of loyalty from the people who work on them. The life can be hard and rough and lonely, yet men put in ten or twenty years on the one station, loving it as if it was their own. I read the other day of an old man who worked his life out on one place and his wages would have been a mere pittance, but he saved what he could and when he died he left it to the station owner. That would be carrying it to an extreme, but to me it epitomises the loyalty the old-timers felt for their station, and in spite of the life being less isolated and rugged today, it's still there to a lesser degree. Lecture over—sorry if I bored you.'

Katriona's blue eyes were shining as she listened avidly. This was what she wanted to learn. 'Please go on, Tay. I'm not bored. Oh, how could you suggest such a thing!'

'You'll have to ask Morgan the rest, we're nearly back at the yards. Ah, look at those blighters, every time they nip off up there in that gut, and it takes a devil of a time to get them back with the dogs.'

Katriona sat fascinated as he worked and whistled his dogs, with infinite patience moving the errant half dozen sheep slowly step by step until they turned and scampered and slid down the steep bank to rejoin the others. As they drew closer to the shed she tried to calm the whirlwind of emotions swirling through her heart and mind, the excitement and anticipation of her next encounter with Morgan, the joy and happiness of being here and the sadness at the thought of leaving.

As Tay let her down by the yards he reminded her, 'You haven't eaten yet. Go and get your breakfast.'

'I'm not hungry,' Katriona replied.

'Tut-tut, that's a really bad sign. One of the worst,' he shook his head warningly at her, his meaning unmistakable.

'Blood and sand! I should have known never to trust a man!' Katriona stormed off towards the homestead, Tay's laughter following her down the road.

She kicked a stone and hurt her toe, then the humour of it struck her, and she swung around and waved at Tay. Her merry laughter rang out to join his. 'Thank you for taking me. I loved it. I love you.'

He waved and she knew he understood. As she turned back she realised Morgan was standing at the fence near her and he was scowling.

'Quite a lad, our Tay!' he said sarcastically.

'Isn't he just?' Katriona was bubbling over with happiness 'He's going to take me up to the tops.'

'The hell he is! When I decide you can go up the tops I'll take you. Is that understood?'

'Yes, all ... all right,' Katriona was bewildered by his anger, her long dark eyelashes fluttered nervously. 'I'll tell Tay I'm not allowed to go with him.'

'You won't, I will.' Morgan yelled at her as he stepped over the yard fence and moved in a direct line to where Tay was putting the sheep through the gate.

Katriona watched them from a distance, hesitating as to whether to go back and protest at Morgan's rudeness. Why was he so upset? Tay was only being kind to her. Yet Tay had said that he had a gut feeling that Morgan would object. Perhaps only the manager was supposed to take you up the tops, and Tay knew that he would be usurping Morgan's prerogative if he took Katriona. Satisfied that she had the answer, she turned once more for the house.

She paused for a moment at the white wrought-iron gate under the shade of the silver birch tree, listening to its leaves rustling in the light breeze, trying to see if it made the same impression on her as it had yesterday afternoon. And it did. She felt again that acute pain as she gazed at the white walls and the roses, the neat concrete paths and green lawns, the riot of colour from the wall of flowers behind the shed, the cool fountain and the purple shadowed hill. All this could have been hers. She could have grown up here, warm, secure and loved. The thought burned her.

Then she thought of Ena McIlroy, who had loved her and cared enough for her to break a promise, and the pain edged away. Suddenly Ena seemed very close to her, Ena's lovely old face full of loving and kindness, her eyes clear and serene, her snow-white hair neatly caught at the nape of her neck. Ena had, by breaking her promise, given Katriona a father and given her this month to learn and to love and to know this place. She had given her a background. Katriona closed her eyes for a second. 'Thank you, God, for giving me a friend like Ena.'

As soon as she had said the words she knew how Ena had made the decision. Whenever the old lady had had a problem, either her own or someone else's, she would tie on her scarf and walk to the kirk to 'have a wee talk with the Lord'. Katriona was sure that there had been many 'wee talks' before Ena had made her decision. And Ena's other saying was, 'If it's well with the Lord it nae matters what other folk think.'

'Katriona, come in and meet some friends,' Mrs Niven was calling to her from the ranchslider doors.

It took Katriona a moment to collect her thoughts and hurry forward. She felt positively scruffy in her overalls and shirt and her hair was ruffled and windblown, and she had no make-up to give her courage. What a mess to be introduced as Ross Carmichael's daughter! Her small chin went up and she stepped lightly into the room ... after she had thought proudly, 'I am his only daughter'.

There seemed to be a roomful of women and children. Mrs Niven touched Katriona lightly on the shoulder. 'Katriona Carmichael, ladies, Ross's daughter. I know you'll all be as thrilled as I am to meet her and to have her staying here for a while.'

Katriona felt warmed by the style of the introduction. 'Now, Katriona, you've been out and about this morning and may have already met some of these ladies' husbands. I was telling them just now that you were so eager to look at the station that you've not yet had your breakfast. This is Mrs Price, our cook.'

Katriona shook hands with a tall, slender, fair-haired woman, and found herself smiling back as she met the warmth in the merry brown eyes.

'Did you meet my Alan? He's the head tractor driver.'

Katriona shook her head. 'No, but I saw him drive out this morning.' Mrs Price sat down and Katriona shook hands with the next person at the table, a young attractive girl of about eighteen. 'I'm Penny, up here cooking for the contract fencers. You can't have met my husband because I haven't caught one yet.'

'Don't get up, Nan,' Mrs Niven spoke hastily to a young woman across the table holding a bright-eyed little girl. 'Katriona, meet Nanette Mason and her daughter Alita, just one year old last week.'

Katriona leaned across to shake hands and touched the baby Alita lightly on the cheek.

'Watch out!' cautioned Nanette. 'She's got eight teeth and can use them.'

'Thanks for the warning, but she doesn't look dangerous.'

'She can be, very. You won't have met my husband Murray because he's driven the truck through to Christchurch and won't be back till late this afternoon.'

'Nanette and Murray board the schoolteacher,' Mrs Niven explained.

Katriona had wanted to meet everyone who was on the station, but not all at once. This was becoming an ordeal and she would never remember all their names.

'You must be positively wilting. Here's a cup of coffee to sustain you. I'm ...'

'Amber!' Katriona cried joyfully, knowing she could not be wrong. Amber had brilliant glowing green eyes, thick dark hair, cut short and shaped to her head like a helmet, dimples which came and went bewitchingly. She looked about eighteen, not old enough to have children.

'You've met my husband Tay—the handsomest man on Evangeline?'

'I have indeed, and he certainly is,' Katriona agreed.

'And the nicest man on the whole station,' Amber prompted.

'Oh, without doubt!' Katriona agreed again with even more enthusiasm, and laughed delightedly.

Amber laughed with her. 'Obviously you have exquisite taste, excellent judgment and are very astute. If Tay had a twin brother, I'd give him to you, but alas, he's an only son.'

'He would have to be identical in every way, before I would have accepted him, had he existed,' Katriona told her solemnly.

'Oh, of course. I could have offered you no less than what I have myself. But you will have dinner with us tonight?'

Mrs Niven interrupted, 'Perhaps Morgan may not ...'

'I'm not inviting Morgan, just Katriona.' Amber's eyes danced with devilment. 'She can't be stuck with Morgan every night. She must have some fun.'

'I accept with gratitude,' Katriona hastily assured her.

'I somehow thought you might.' Amber's mobile features moved from an enchanting smile to intense concentration. 'I did bring him with me, I'm sure.'

'If you're looking for Jordan he's under the table,' Nanette offered.

'Thanks a million.' Amber bent under the table and dragged out a little boy of about three years old. 'Jordan, say hello to Katriona.' Jordan gave Katriona a long silent unwavering stare, then disappeared back under the table. Amber shrugged her shoulders. 'Win some, lose some.'

Katriona sat down and drank her coffee. It was delicious.

'How many station men did you meet this morning?' Nanette asked.

'Just Morgan and Tay to speak to,' Katriona admitted.

'Poor you. Not a great deal of choice really. Wait till you meet my husband, Murray.'

Amber's eyes glittered. 'Poor man, he'll fail to make any impression, I assure you, Katriona. Once you've met the best, everyone else is second class.'

'Just what do you mean by that, Amber?' Nanette demanded.

'There's the mail, girls,' Mrs Niven announced in what Katriona guessed were tones of heartfelt relief. 'Come on, we'll open the bag. Come along, Katriona, come and share some of our excitement. The mail and milk and groceries arrive three days a week and it's always a thrill. The children come up from the school, and quite often the men are in. When you live in an isolated community, not going off the station for weeks, you really look forward to a change and news of the outside world. Watch the children's faces light up when their name is called.'

'Do they get mail regularly?' Katriona asked in surprise as they followed the women down the path.

'Usually. All their school work is done by correspondence, all written down and sent to Wellington each fortnight. They write to their teachers and the teachers write back to them and they're really close. In fact I would say those teachers are closer to the outback children's lives than their counterparts in the city schools who see their twenty or thirty children each day but never know them. They haven't got the time, perhaps.'

Glancing back as she got to the gate, Katriona smiled to see Amber dragging Jordan out from under the table by one arm and a leg. She was certainly winning this one! Suddenly Jordan let go and he and Amber toppled over on the carpet in the sunshine, a bundle of arms, legs, and laughter. Katriona saw her scoop the little boy into her arms to hug and kiss him, and then bearing him aloft like some miniature weightlifter she ran through the gate Katriona held open for her.

Amber dropped Jordan to his feet and gasped, 'I lose all the battles at adult level with Jordan, but when I get down to kid level, weight for age I win handsomely. Here's my car, hop in and watch the proceedings . . . no extra charge.'

Katriona sat down thankfully. There were so many people around that she could not face any more introductions. She did not want to lose the names she already had. Perhaps Amber had known that. Katriona closed her eyes, just for a moment.

'Here's Jordan.' Amber opened the door and dumped him on Katriona's knee. 'I'll run you up to my place so you'll know where to find it tonight. It will only take a couple of minutes. Okay? Oh, here's my daughter Tania and my son Eden. Meet Katriona, children. Now off you go in the truck with Dad.'

Katriona, half asleep, grabbed the small packet of dynamite named Jordan, then smiled at Tania, only having time to note the slender brown grace and the transparent honesty and trust in her eyes, the same mountain-clear look her father Tay had. Then her attention riveted on Eden, a strikingly handsome boy with grey eyes and thick dark hair . . . he was the living image of Morgan. She felt a cold hand clutch her heart, and almost choked as the ugly thought touched her mind. She rejected it instantly and said quietly, 'Lovely children, Amber. And I love their names.'

'Yes, they are,' Amber said softly. 'Real chip off the old block, Eden, spitting image of his father.'

Katriona searched the liquid depths of those taunting green eyes, and knew that this was some sort of a test, and that she did not want to fail. She closed her eyes for a second before saying carefully, 'He doesn't look like Tay from where I sit.'

'Are you stating a fact or asking a question?' The green eyes flashed twin fires.

It was not going to be an easy test. Katriona sighed, 'Both.'

'You want an answer?'

'Yes,' Katriona replied honestly.

'You wouldn't like to hazard a guess?' There was a challenge.

'No. And I'm tired.'

'He's not Morgan's child. His father was Eden, a cousin of Morgan's. He was killed in a car accident three months after we were married. I came here to visit Morgan and met Tay, and we were married. Sorry to do that to you, but I had to know you as a person. Mostly I let people get on with their own vivid imaginings, but I wanted to be friends with you.'

Katriona put Jordan down carefully on the seat and got out of the car. 'We'll be friends. I know where your house is ... I'll see you at seven.'

'You're mad at me, redheaded mad.' Amber laughed wickedly. 'Why did you reject the obvious? For Morgan's honour? For mine? For Tay's?' The green eyes were soft and tender. 'You fool, to let yourself love him like that.'

'You should be burned at the stake for being a green-eyed witch,' Katriona said flatly. She stalked up the path, passing Morgan without speaking. She grabbed her towel and dressing-gown from her room and hurried to the bath-room to shower and wash her hair. She wasn't used to the heat. She chose a lilac silk dress to put on later and lay down on her bed. She was drained of all emotion, yet over-full of emotion. She wanted quiet and peace just for a short while. She was not even angry that both Tay and Amber had guessed her secret; they were perceptive, and she knew she could trust them.

'Lunch-time!' Morgan shouted, and rapped on the door.

Katriona's eyes flicked open wide. How awful! She must have dropped off to sleep as soon as she lay down. Then she saw by her watch that it had only been for half an hour and was relieved. Quickly she brushed her hair into its natural free-flowing waves and slipped on her dress and sandals, then hurried to the dining-room.

'Sorry for being late, Mrs Niven. May I do anything to help?' Katriona avoided looking at Morgan who was seated at the table.

Mrs Niven smiled, 'Call me Nivvy, they all do. And sit down. We only have a light lunch, salad and cold meat, usually about twelve, but Morgan had some office work to do, so we decided to let you have forty winks. Do you feel better?'

'Like a giant refreshed.' She sat by Morgan, telling herself that she would get used to sitting close to him. And it was only a matter of time before this feeling that her bones were melting would disappear. She turned from him to gaze out the sliding doors to the garden and beyond to the Hope River and to her special mountain, incredibly beautiful in the afternoon heat.

'Your tea, Katriona, and pass this one on to Morgan. Help yourself to sauce, pickles or whatever. You must be hungry, you've had nothing all day. The sauce is really good this year, I'm very pleased with it.'

Katriona placed Morgan's cup of tea carefully beside him, unexpectedly touching his arm after she had put it down. She flinched as if she had touched a live electric wire. She knew he was just sitting there watching her, but she would not look at him. It was an outright lie that she would ever get used to sitting beside him ... it would not matter if he sat at the other side of the table, or twenty feet away from her. He was one of those men who had such magnetic maleness that you were conscious of it a mile away.

'Enjoyed your morning, Katriona?' Morgan asked with a hint of amusement behind the words.

She made herself meet his gaze directly, and ignored the laughter there. 'Fine. It was a grand morning, and the trip with Tay was well worth the whole flight to New Zealand.'

Nivvy chatted on, completely unaware of the tension at the other end of the table. 'Tay is nice, really nice, and a good head shepherd. Isn't that so, Morgan?'

'Certainly is, Nivvy. Good at his job, and other things.' His words were casual, but his eyes were wickedly telling Katriona that he knew exactly the effect he was having on her and that he was enjoying every minute of it.

Katriona forced herself to hold his eyes coolly and levelly for one second longer, then thankfully switched her attention to Mrs Niven. 'Did you make all the sauces and pickles yourself, Nivvy?'

'Yes. You must come out to the store room, it's brim full of preserves, nearly three hundred bottles.'

'We'll never get through three hundred bottles of tomato sauce, Nivvy,' Morgan teased her.

'Ah, Morgan, you know better than that. Take no notice of him, Katriona, he loves to tease.'

'Torment,' Katriona snapped, then bit her lip, angry that she had given him that much evidence of his success. 'How long does it take for an airmail letter to get here from Scotland, please, Nivvy?'

'Oh, about a week, I would say.'

'Yes, you should hear from the faithful Donald within a week,' Morgan offered.

'I hope so,' Katriona replied fervently. 'He said he would write as soon as I left, and it seems a long time since I was with him.'

'A friend of yours?' Nivvy asked with real interest.

'A very close friend of Katriona's.' Morgan's voice was mocking. 'I met him when I was over there—a pleasant fellow. He wasn't happy at losing her to New Zealand even for a short time. He wants to marry her and she could hardly tear herself from his side.'

Katriona threw him a withering look and concentrated on her lunch.

'That's lovely. Still, I'm glad you came. Ross needed to see you.'

Katriona smiled at Nivvy. 'And I needed to see him. It's a pity that he has to be away this week.'

'Never mind, Morgan will take you about with him. He knows this place almost as well as Ross. You're not wearing an engagement ring, Katriona?'

'I don't believe in them, neither does Donald. A wide gold wedding ring is sufficient.' That should hold Morgan Grant, she thought viciously, as she took another careful mouthful.

'He should be able to afford a really pricey one when Ross coughs up.' The silky sarcastic whisper did not reach Nivvy, but it hit Katriona like a slap on the face and she choked. She knew Morgan enjoyed slapping her on the back with unnecessary force.

She stood up, still coughing. The tears in her eyes were not from choking but from pure unadulterated temper. 'I'll get a glass of water.'

She went round the room divider and took a glass from the cupboard and slowly filled it with water. She wondered how long you had to spend in jail in New Zealand for cold-blooded murder.

An open sports car roared up the hill and braked directly in front of the wrought iron gate, and Katriona saw Carla swing her long shapely legs over the low door without bothering to open it. Dressed in white short shorts, a white swathed scarf for a top and white sandals, she drew every eye. Her long blonde hair fell like a golden river down her back and her superbly shaped body, tanned a glorious even brown, was worth a second look.

She stopped by the gate, flung her hair back arrogantly, and posed casually, almost as if to let everyone look their fill and dare to find fault, then she sauntered up the path.

'The devil!' Morgan slapped the table and went to meet her.

'Not quite, but close,' Nivvy remarked crisply. She joined Katriona by the kitchen window for a moment. 'It was too much to hope she would leave us in peace. Oh, well, coffee for one coming up.'

Katriona's eyes narrowed as she watched Morgan meet Carla, and thought bitterly that they were made for each other. A pair of superb animals—whoops, human beings—well, specimens was closer maybe. Morgan was standing there, tall, incredibly good-looking, his dark head slightly bent to hear what Carla was saying, a half smile on his face. And Carla, in high-heeled sandals almost as tall as he, her exquisite face turned to his, taking the full afternoon sunshine square on her face without fear, talking fast to him with the ease of a long acquaintance, made Katriona wince and turn away. Amber was right ... it was foolish of her to love Morgan, and worse to be so weak that she could not stop herself from loving him.

'Shall I get some meat out, and more bread for Carla?' she asked Nivvy.

'Huh! That one has only a coffee for breakfast, coffee for lunch because she has to be so careful of the figure divine. She'd put weight on if she so much as smelled a slice of bread. Do you have to watch what you eat?'

'No. It doesn't seem to matter what I eat, I still look like a broomstick,' Katriona told her with a rueful grin.

'Thought so,' Nivvy said with satisfaction. 'The way you downed that meal last night did my soul good. It would have slowed up a good shearer and you never blinked. What's the use of good cooking if people will only gnaw on a carrot and munch a lettuce leaf? As for being a broomhandle, fiddlesticks. You've all the slender grace of a hind and all the necessary equipment to stand any man on his ear, if only you'd learn to use it. Why don't you practise on Morgan? Give him something else to think of besides Carla's overblown, over-cultivated charm.'

Katriona stood stock still, her lips parted in silent protest and honest bewilderment.

Nivvy yelled unceremoniously through the window, 'Coffee poured, Carla!' then turned abruptly on Katriona. 'That one would make a down payment of a million dollars to have a shape like yours. Believe me, I know what I'm talking about. Go to it! Shake Morgan out of his senses, you can do it.'

'You're crazy!' Katriona's voice wobbled and she half laughed at the absurdity of the suggestion. 'I don't want to, even if I could, which I couldn't. Donald loves me.'

Nivvy sniffed. 'Sorry, I forgot about him. What a pity! Mustn't be up to much, though, if he didn't tell you you were beautiful.'

Katriona blushed scarlet.

'Oh, he did, and you didn't believe him ... what a silly child you are!'

Carla swept into the room and faced Katriona. 'Sorry about last night. Came as a bit of a shock, it really did.' She turned her back and sat down with studied grace, patting the seat beside her. 'Come and sit beside me, Morgan, while I have my coffee.'

'Sorry, I can't. I'm late, Carla. I have to get over to the woolshed.' He was already half out of the door.

She was on her feet in an instant and caught him as he went down the path. 'May I borrow the Mustang? My car has a tiny, tiny squeak in it. Be a pet?'

Katriona craned her head to see Morgan's face. He was not pleased. He hesitated a minute. 'Okay, the keys are in the study.'

'Could you get what's-his-name to check my car out?' Carla called as he got to the gate.

'No, I could not. What's-his-name is too busy on farm work showering sheep at present and he has a ton of farm machinery to keep moving. His name is Tim and it's time you learnt it. Get your garage to check your car, or buy a new one.' He walked away.

Nivvy winked at Katriona and licked her finger chalking an imaginary mark on the wall.

Carla wore a petulant expression on her face when she returned, but it cleared as she finished her coffee. 'I'm going into Hanmer, Katriona. Would you like a trip with me?'

'No, thank you. I would rather just wander around the station,' Katriona answered politely, trying to disguise her surprise.

'You can do that any time. It's less than half an hour each way, and you should know where your nearest village is. Quite apart from that, it's a lovely day and Hanmer is perfect at this time of the year. Do come! It will make me feel you've forgiven me for my bad manners last night.'

'There's nothing to forgive,' Katriona said, still not wanting to go, but feeling it was churlish to refuse.

Nivvy spoke quickly, 'Oh, Carla, if you're going into Hanmer, could you get me some pears? Mandy rang to say the wind had shaken her pear tree and the ground is covered. They'll rot if no one takes them. Take two cases with you when you go. Thank you.'

Carla frowned, then her face changed to a charming smile. 'You'll get your pears if Katriona comes with me. She can pick them while I dash about the shops. That's settled, then.' She picked up her bag and left the room, calling over her shoulder, 'I'll be staying the night, of course.'

'Of course,' Nivvy repeated with a different inflection in her voice. 'Sorry about that, Katriona. Mandy is my friend and she works, so there'll be no one there to help you. The children will be away at school. When Carla drops you off, just pick up the pears from the ground, don't take any bruised ones, and top the box up from the tree if there's not enough fallen. It should only take you about ten minutes.'

'What if they come home while I'm there? They'll think I'm stealing them.'

'Just say you came from Evangeline and you are picking

them for me.' Nivvy looked sympathetic, 'You'd better get used to the idea that Carla usually gets her own way, although it bothers me why she wants to take you ... she rarely offers to take me or any of the other women. I wish Morgan was here ...' her voice trailed away nervously.

'Think she'll do me an injury?' Katriona suggested with a giggle. 'Bang me on the head and railroad me home to Scotland?'

'Oh, no. She might get blood on her clothes ... or break a fingernail.' Nivvy hurried to answer the phone ringing out in the study, and came back moments later. 'Ross wants to talk to you, Katriona.'

Colour washed over her face, leaving it pale as she hurried through to take the call. She still was not used to having a father, let alone talking to him. She picked up the phone gingerly. 'Hello!'

'That you, Katriona? Your father here. I have a few spare minutes and thought I'd call you with an idea I had. I'm missing a quarter of your visit, so if I ring you each night and we have a chat we'll be part way along the path of getting to know each other by the time I get back. Just a few minutes, and you can tell me what you've been doing so I can follow your progress. What do you think of that for an idea? Be honest.'

'I'm always honest,' Katriona answered. 'I like your idea just fine. I appreciate your kindness, but won't it be very expensive?'

'Not so expensive as ringing you in Scotland if I want to chat with you next month. So what have you done this morning and what do you plan for this afternoon?'

'I went with Tay to bring in the sheep from the clover paddock and saw turkeys and geese that were allowed to ... er ... range free. And I saw a tiny lake and Maid, Tay's dog, working the sheep and a mountain called Skiddaw which Tay called a hill. Carla is taking me to Hanmer now and I'm to pick some pears for Nivvy while I'm there.'

'Great, that's what I want to hear, that you're getting about, seeing things, learning things. What about Morgan?

Didn't you see him today? Doesn't he rate a mention?'

'He spoiled my sunrise this morning,' Katriona told him indignantly, and heard a roar of laughter from the other end of the line.

'Blotted his copybook already, has he? I'll ring you to-morrow night. Till then, take care, my girl.'

Katriona looked resentfully at the phone. Ross had gone without giving her a chance to say goodbye, and she had been enjoying talking to him. With sudden insight she knew he was as nervous as she was in the present situation, and the knowledge lifted her heart. Anyone scared of damaging a relationship must value that relationship. Perhaps her father was not truly indifferent to her existence.

'Come on, Katriona, don't dawdle,' Carla snapped at her. 'Pick up the boxes as you come through the kitchen.' Katriona followed the briskly moving Carla, wishing even more that she was not going with her. Nivvy winked as she handed her the empty fruit boxes, humming a tune loudly which Katriona instantly recognised as 'Onward Christian Soldiers', and grinned.

Carla reached an implement shed across the yard which had a bright yellow fastback car parked beside a motor-boat on a trailer. She flung the door open, waved Katriona forward impatiently. 'Throw those boxes in the back, and for goodness' sake hurry up!'

Katriona had been hesitating because it appeared to her that Carla had got into the passenger seat. As she sat down she asked, 'What make of car is it?'

'American make, a Mustang, fabulous car really, left-hand drive, of course, and a ton of power, but a breeze to drive. Twin carbs, custom-built—just feel the leather! Mmmm! I love speed, and this car holds the road as if it was married to it, a hundred is just idling along.'

Curiously Katriona watched Carla's face as she switched on the key and the powerful motor sprang to life. Carla reversed out expertly into the yard and swung wide to take the corner by the diesel pumps, then picked up speed going down the bluff. For the first time she seemed alive, excited and happy as if she were part of the power that moved the huge car.

As they turned on to the main Lewis Pass highway and headed east, Carla's foot went down and the car responded instantly, gathering speed as they hurtled up around the hill above Horseshoe Lake, which sat like a beautiful bluey-green jewel in its tranquil mountain setting. It looked so cool in the burning afternoon heat, surrounded as it was with green flax and raupo reeds and floating snowy-plumed toi-toi.

The windows were down and Carla's long blonde hair was swept back from her shoulders, and her smile was one of pure delight. Katriona was not scared of speed, in fact she was almost unaware of it until she saw the speedometer creeping up and up, and even then she was not worried. Carla handled the car with easy unconcerned confidence.

The speed was too fast for Katriona to enjoy the scenery, just time to grab at the flashes of beauty, the hills brown and golden, the river green and clear, a cabbage tree in flower on the hillside, and the distant mountains. They roared by the slower traffic, and followed the winding road over white-painted bridges, round steep rising bluffs and hills, and swooped down gorges and gullies. Katriona was content to see a new aspect of Carla's character, and was pleased at least to find something to admire even if she could not share it.

'Hanmer coming up. I have to stop at the pottery shop, come in if you want to, though I shan't be long.' Carla eased back the speed and drifted in beside a small building at the road junction.

Needing no second bidding, Katriona followed her through the door. It was not a large shop, just a counter at one end and display shelves all along one wall. Several people were browsing or buying.

'Damn! I didn't think they'd be busy. I hate waiting,' Carla snapped.

Katriona hid her grin. She was quite happy to have a little time to see the display. She wandered to the shelves and tried to imagine that she had a purse full of money and could buy what she wanted. Which would she choose? The jug and bowl? The casserole? The ashtray? No, there was something special about the shape and design of the cream jug and sugar bowl which caught and held her attention. She narrowed her choice down to two designs, autumn-toned open leaves fantastically arranged in a sunburst flower pattern on a white background, or the same pattern repeated in a greeny-blue colour on white.

She took the autumn-coloured bowl from the shelf, and loved the smooth silky finish of the work, the feel of the shape in her hands, the whorls inside even and perfect, clay from the potter's hand, turned into this bowl.

'You like that one?' A man with glasses and an apron splattered with clay marks spoke to her.

'You made this?' Katriona's voice always went husky when she was deeply moved. 'Why, it's fine ... it's fine.' Such an understated compliment for all the skill and care which had gone into making the bowl, all the artistry. She replaced the bowl and picked up the matching jug and her palms caressed it lovingly, feeling its warmth and shape and beauty. 'It's lovely, and I would love to take it, but I haven't got my purse with me.'

'You'll be this way again?' The man did not seem to be upset, and smiled when Katriona nodded. 'Next time you call I'll take you out the back and show you the whole process from the rough clay we buy in to the finished work you hold there in your hand.'

'Do come, Katriona!' Carla's sharp voice shattered the moment and Katriona carefully replaced the jug and turned to the man.

'I really would love to do that. Thank you very much for inviting me.'

Carla was furiously impatient. 'Really, so stupid ... that woman took simply ages to choose a coffee mug set, dithering around. I just came in to grab something for an engagement present, anything would have done. I should have been served immediately. Why people are so gone on this stuff beats me!'

Carla did not bother to lower her voice and Katriona winced at the words hoping the man had not heard, and followed Carla to the car. 'May I see what you chose?'

'There on the seat, a set of coffee mugs in that blue colour. I could have been in and out in a couple of minutes if that wretched woman hadn't been so indecisive. Everyone has gone mad over this pottery ware. Amber has her place loaded with the stuff and is always buying more. It's a disease with her.'

Katriona giggled. It would be with Amber. She would appreciate the skill and loving craftsmanship which went into making these lovely things, and she would treasure them. Perhaps Amber would bring her back one afternoon and they could stay as long as they wanted.

She recognised the Hanmer village from the tourist book photographs she had studied back in Scotland and knew that it had not exaggerated the charm of the attractively laid out township with its tree-lined streets glorious in their autumn beauty.

'Right, you pick the pears, I'll be back.' Carla pulled into a drive and leaned over to toss out the boxes. 'Get a move on. I won't be long.'

'All charm, that one,' muttered Katriona as she watched Carla reverse rapidly out of the drive and sweep away in the big car. She laughed out loud as she realised that all unconsciously she had caught Nivvy's way of thinking of Carla as 'that one'. It suited Carla. Fancy not having the time to enjoy anything in life except her personal appearance, men and fast cars! Katriona still wondered why she had been invited. Perhaps she was misjudging Carla and she did mean to be kind, and it was just her unfortunate manner which was off-putting.

Revelling in the heat of the afternoon sun striking through her silk dress, Katriona gasped as she saw the green lawn, a mass of large ripe golden pears, and the tree above so laden that it was hard to see where they had

fallen from. It took her about five minutes to fill each case
and still there was fruit on the ground. She carried the
boxes over to the edge of the drive ready for Carla, then
catching sight of a rubber swimming pool she wandered
over. It would be nice to plunge into the cool water, but
she rapidly changed her mind as she saw three small trout
and a slinky snaky eel basking in the sunwarmed water. As
she touched the side, they flashed for cover under three or
four bunches of river weed floating on the surface. The
children of the house might enjoy swimming with their
pets, but Katriona was not too keen.

How long was 'not long' to Carla? Katriona wandered
about the garden admiring the apple trees bending their
branches with an abundance of fruit. It was so hot. The sun
was inviting, and the hedges around the property gave
plenty of privacy and there was no one at home, so why not
sunbathe? Quickly she stripped off her dress and picking
some juicy pears from the ground stretched out to let the
hot sun beat down on her. An hour passed as she lay first
on her back, then on her stomach. She knew she would not
burn, she was one of those rare redheads whose skin
tanned easily and evenly. Her skin would be a nice smooth
even gold by the time she went back to Scotland. Maybe
she had inherited from her father her ability to brown
without burning, something to do with the pigmentation of
her skin. She certainly had not got it from her mother, who
was a traditional peaches and cream beauty and who was
most careful of her complexion, never allowing the sun's
rays to touch her cheeks.

Nice to have something of her father in her and to be
able to recognise it. Another hour, another pear, a cloudless
blue sky above and time to dream ... of Morgan ... Morgan back there in the mountains, with the sheep and the
tussock and the tall trees, and the deer ... anyone can
dream ... dream that he was kind ... that he liked her
... that she could talk with him in that easy intimate way
which Nivvy and Carla used ... that she could know him.

Reality was the urgent roar of the Mustang engine revving up the street, and Katriona slipped on her dress and wiped the pear juice from her face. The trip back was fast, but not as fast as the outward journey, and it was obvious that Carla had something on her mind. She put Katriona through a third-degree questioning session and was not pleased with Katriona's ability to skilfully field and avoid the more searching personal ones.

'I must take you up to see the new house,' Carla told her. 'Such a pity you'll be gone long before it's completed. It's truly a magnificent wedding present to give Morgan and me. But then I could expect it, because he's always treated me as his own daughter.'

Stupidly Katriona's eyes went to Carla's left hand. 'You're engaged to Morgan?'

'Oh, don't look for the ring. I hate long formal engagements, so we've dispensed with that part.'

Fiercely Katriona wanted to refute the fact that Morgan and Carla were to marry. After all, only at lunch time she herself had pretended that she didn't want an engagement ring to cover the fact that she did not have one. 'I thought that was Ross's own house, the new one.'

'Ross is building it, but he let me work with the architects to plan it, because Morgan and I will be living there more than he will. He has his own self-contained flat in the house, of course. You must ask him to show you the plans. I'm very proud of them, most ingenious.'

Rebelliously Katriona wanted to shout at Carla that ingenious meant clever and inventive, and that described Carla and her fake engagement. She wanted to shout at Carla that she, Katriona, was Ross's real daughter, not an *as if* daughter. She did not do that because the truth was that Ross had probably treated Carla as his daughter and it was more than probable that Morgan was to marry Carla, and wishing it was not so would not alter that fact. Carla would not lie about anything that was so easy to verify. Katriona only had to ask Morgan ... and she knew she never would.

It was pure delight to see the homestead and buildings

of Evangeline lying in the sun so beautifully as they rounded the hill above Horseshoe Lake. Only a day here and she felt she was coming home.

At the mail box Carla got out and checked for parcels and messages to take up to the house. She seemed a long time. Katriona sat feasting her eyes with all the beauty in front of her, the station buildings, the long line of the Frenchman's Plantation piercing the blue sky, the hills, and back beyond to the mountains. She was now able to match up some of the people she had met this morning with the neat green and white farm cottages, she could hear the dogs barking and the men whistling to them, and her heartbeat speeded up as she knew she was getting closer to Morgan.

Suddenly Carla jerked open the door by Katriona. 'Move over quickly, please.'

Katriona automatically responded to the sharp order and shifted across the seat, and to her surprise Carla slipped into the passenger seat, leaving Katriona behind the wheel.

'When I was talking to Ross on the phone last night he said he'd ordered a small car for you while you were here. But Morgan said you can't drive. It seems such a shame, owning a brand new car and not having the pleasure of driving it. So he was really pleased when I offered to teach you.'

'In this ... this monster!' Katriona was aghast. 'I couldn't! The hood is five miles long. I can't even see properly. I'm not ready.'

'I told Morgan that you'd be too chicken to learn, but he said you had more in you than appeared on the surface. Get out, and I'll tell him he was wrong. Ross can cancel the order. Waste of money, really, when you're only here a month, a stupid extravagant gesture.'

'Morgan said that about me?' Katriona sat stunned. Her father was so pleased to have her here he had bought her a new car for just one month. Two bursts of excitement waved through her slender body. If Morgan thought she could do it she would try. '*Can* you teach me to drive this?'

'It's a breeze. I told you it's fully automatic .. no

sweat. Still, if you haven't the nerve to make the effort, what's the point? Get out.'

'I'd be scared of damaging Morgan's car,' Katriona said shakily.

'With me teaching you, you've nothing to worry about. Do you doubt my driving ability?' Carla demanded scathingly.

'No, not really . . .'

'Well then, what have you got to lose? I'll take full responsibility. Switch on. All you have to do is steer the damned thing. Keep the middle black line on the hood in the centre of the road and aim it.'

'I wish I could see a little better.'

'Are you going to have a crack at it or not? Make up your mind. We can't spend the night here.'

Katriona's chin went up. 'Don't bully me. Tell me what to do.' She was scared to death, and so intent on watching the road and gripping the steering wheel that she did not see the slow satisfied smile of triumph spread across Carla's face. She followed Carla's instructions exactly, and the car moved slowly forward . . . it seemed too wide for the road, but Carla leaned across and guided it through the gateway. As they crept along the flat road, ever so slowly, Katriona managed to keep the centre mark in the centre of the road and felt she was not doing too badly.

'Great! You're doing fine. Now, push the accelerator down a bit more. Don't be frightened. I'll take over if need be.' The car surged forward and Carla's hand shot out again to steady the wheel. 'See, it's quite simple really. All you need is confidence. Ross and Morgan will be so pleased with you.'

Katriona was thrilled that she had got this far without mishap. She also was feeling guilty for not trusting Carla. She was really being very patient and kind.

'Okay, now here's the hill. We'll need a bit more speed. You've got to gun her a bit to make it. Stick your foot down or you'll stall the damned thing.'

Katriona instinctively obeyed, trusting Carla completely,

and the next few seconds became a nightmare. She heard
Carla laughing wildly as the powerful car leaped forward,
spurting gravel, and she fought desperately to hold it on the
steep narrow metal road. As they topped the rise of the hill,
the yard was full of men, trucks, children, motor-bikes,
dogs and the sheep streaming from the sheepyards. There
was nowhere to go, and she had no idea how to stop the
car. She felt sick with the thought of what was going to
happen. In that instant she knew Carla had done this to her
deliberately.

Carla grabbed the wheel, deftly flicking it one way and
then the other to dodge the sheep, dogs, vehicles, and
people. With consummate skill she seemed to be going to
drive right through the confusion without accident. Then
there was a terrible grinding, wrenching, tearing sound as
they ran over a hastily abandoned farm bike, and then on to
wing an old car parked by the gate, before Carla switched
off the engine and applied the brake.

Katriona just sat there shaking with shock until her
door was thrown open, and Morgan reached in and jerked
her bodily from the seat. 'What the hell do you think you're
doing, you crazy female? You could have killed someone!
You complete idiot, you've smashed my car, and young
Gary's—look at them!'

He shouted and yelled at her, and shook her as if she was
a rag doll, but Katriona did not care. She wished he would
kill her. She had been such a fool.

'That will do, Morgan. She's had enough. Let's get to
the bottom of this.' Tay's voice was quiet, yet it stopped
Morgan, and he released Katriona. She would have fallen
except that Tay put his arms around her. 'Okay, you guys,
the excitement is over. Get those sheep away, Murray. Tim,
clear the bike away and tow Gary's bomb out of here.
Nobody's hurt, so back to work.'

As if viewing him from a distance, Katriona saw Morgan
through the tears which slid down her cheeks walking
round his car examining the damage. She saw Nivvy stand-

ing by the gate, her hand to her mouth, and she saw Carla smiling.

Morgan's voice cracked like a whiplash. 'Carla. You have an explanation?'

Wiping the smile from her face, Carla turned to face Morgan, her expression contrite and pleading. 'Oh, Morgan, please forgive me for being such a fool. I shouldn't have listened to Katriona. Honestly, when I told her that Ross was sending up a new car for her, she nagged me all the way to Hanmer and back to teach her to drive. She nearly drove me crazy. She insisted that you wouldn't mind her learning in your car . . . But I did have my doubts, really I did.' The lying smooth voice went on and on, and Katriona buried her face in Tay's comforting shoulder trying to blot out the pain of knowing how badly she had been tricked.

'Well, she finally pulled rank, and said she was Ross's daughter and that you were only the manager and that you'd been instructed by Ross to see that she had everything she wanted while she was here. Okay, so I was foolish to give in, but she'd been on my back for hours. I thought she couldn't do much damage between here and the gate if she just crawled along, and I could steer if I had to . . . Damn it all, Morgan, she wouldn't listen to me. She knew it all. I've had a fright too. We nearly went over the bank coming up the hill.'

'Oh, stop crying, Carla. I hate crying women, so you can turn off the waterworks. They don't impress me.'

Katriona immediately scrubbed the tears from her face and pushed herself away from Tay. She must stand on her own feet, and take what was coming to her. It took courage, but she turned to face Morgan, her chin held high, but defeat in her blue eyes.

'Have you anything to say for yourself, Katriona Carmichael?' Morgan was blazing mad, his grey eyes flashing fires of fury. It was obvious he believed Carla. Anything Katriona said would sound pathetic against that carefully planned story. Against the anger and accusation in his face, she quailed.

'Nothing.'

'Not even an apology?'

Katriona swallowed nervously, feeling perspiration beading her forehead. 'You believe Carla's story?'

'Have you got a better one?'

'No.'

'You risk the lives of almost everyone on the station and you've got nothing to say. As long as you had your fun it doesn't matter if sheep or dogs or people are hurt. You've smashed my car, and young Gary's, you've wrecked a farm bike which is worth hundreds of dollars and you stand there like Joan of Arc, apparently considering yourself above suspicion, above criticism. Well, you aren't. Even if you are the boss's daughter I'll tell you what I think of you. I think you're a vain, stupid, frivolous female, who puts her own pleasure ahead of people's lives, and that you're behaving exactly as your mother did when she was here. You disgust me. God help Ross Carmichael!'

Morgan turned on his heel and strode away.

Katriona felt herself floating, swaying gently backwards and forwards like a young poplar in a breeze, the sun bright, then fading into blackness and the sensation of falling.

CHAPTER SIX

'DRINK this.' Amber was sitting beside her on a couch.

'What is it?' Katriona half sat up, brushing her curls back from her face.

'Whisky.' Amber put her arm around Katriona's slender shoulders. 'Tay said I was to give you a whisky straight, and if you don't look any better I was to give you another. Now drink it.'

It was easier to swallow it than argue, so Katriona downed it with a grimace. She felt the spirit burn her mouth and throat, but it failed to warm her. She could not stop shaking. She handed the glass back to Amber. 'Thanks.'

'You don't look much better to me, I'll go and get a refill.' Amber hurried off in spite of Katriona's protests.

'Tay said you had to have it.' Amber was implacable. 'Down the hatch!'

'No,' Katriona refused stubbornly from between chattering teeth.

'If Daddy say we have to do something, we got to do it.'

Katriona looked up to find Tania, Eden and Jordan watching her with interest. She did not know which one had spoken.

'House rule,' said Amber with a smile. 'If Daddy says ...'

Katriona drained the glass silently.

'Good, you're starting to get a bit of colour back. When Tay marched in with you in his arms I thought he had a corpse for me!'

Katriona stopped shaking and knew the whisky was warming her. 'Does he often bring corpses in?'

'Oh, frequently, always young and beautiful ones, but you're the first redheaded one. Makes for a change. I often wonder where he finds them all.'

'This one isn't used to neat whisky. I may end up walking around on the ceiling.'

'Teach the children how to do it. It will keep them amused on wet days.'

Katriona laughed. Amber was very special. 'What does it take to throw you?' she asked.

'Nothing can as long as Tay loves me.' Amber's face creased into a radiant smile.

'I can believe that,' Katriona said as a swift pain of Morgan's hate and anger arrowed through her. She would never know the joy that was so evident on Amber's face.

'Tay's orders were, one whisky, followed by a second if needed, no talk, or even thinking until he gets back. He won't be long. Tania and Eden, finish your homework then do your chores, you can talk to Katriona later. Now, how do I stop you from thinking? Jordan, go and get your play school work and show your paintings to Katriona.' She watched the small boy rush off. 'I defy anyone to think when Jordan demands their attention! He'll be back in a second, so I'll get on with dinner.'

Katriona nodded, happy to be left on her own. The room had a warm, loved feel to it, a family room, reflecting Amber's exciting personality as well as Tay's more steadying influence. The books and record collection would be Tay's, the furniture and furnishings were Amber, so was the cascade of colour from the jar of peacock feathers, the paintings were Amber, the wall plaques Tay, the spinning wheel and the Aran sweater on needles . . .

'Me paintings.' Jordan had a sheaf of papers in his hands. He put them in a pile on the floor and took the first one. 'Woolshed.' He glanced up at Katriona on the couch, then bounced to his feet and caught her hand to pull her down beside him on the carpet. 'See me paintings.'

The invitation was irresistible. Katriona took the large square of white newsprint covered with a mess of black paint. 'Tell me what it is.'

Jordan, spreadeagled on the floor, studied it carefully, then gave her a pitying glance. 'Sheepyards. Daddy 'ere.

Jordan 'ere. Mummy way over 'ere. Tania 'ere. Eden 'ere.'
His grin was appealing and his laughter contagious.

'Where's the woolshed?'

'Sheep 'ere.' Jordan's hand swept the middle of the painting. 'Woolshed 'ere.'

He went through the rest of the paintings the same way.
Katriona wondered if he could really see what he had
painted, so she picked up the discarded black painting.
'Where's Daddy?'

Jordan leaned over it with intense concentration. 'Daddy
'ere. Eden 'ere. Tania 'ere.'

He did know. Katriona giggled. It must be the whisky,
because suddenly she felt happy again, infected by this
small boy's delight in his work. 'Where's Mummy?'

'Mummy gone 'ome,' Jordan stated flatly.

'Mummy over there,' Katriona argued, touching the
painting.

'Mummy not 'ere. Mummy gone 'ome. Truck 'ere.'

Tania and Eden ran in. Eden was always first to speak.
'Do you want to see our pets? We've finished our homework.'

Katriona stood up. 'I'd love to see them. What pets do
you have?'

'Canaries, budgies, goats, deer, sheep, pigs, a rabbit, a
calf . . .' Eden stopped for want of breath.

Tania slipped her hand into Katriona's hand. 'Come and
see Taffy first. He's my budgie, and he can talk.'

Katriona walked through to the kitchen where Amber
was using the cake mixer on the bench and busily wiping
down an array of preserving jars filled with golden pears.
On the room divider were pot plants and some choice pieces
of pottery from the Hanmer shop. Katriona admired Taffy
and was about to speak to Amber when she saw Somali, the
big grey gelding, through the kitchen window. Her face
went still with hurt. It must have been about this time last
evening that Morgan had saved her from the bull, and he
had kissed her. There was no joy in the memory . . . so close
then, so far apart now. He despised her.

'No thinking,' Amber commanded sternly.

'Daddy not 'ere.' Katriona gave a wan smile.

'Daddy soon 'ere. Go and see the rabbit.' Amber also used Jordan's speech pattern.

Outside in a roomy rabbit hutch was an enormous fluffy white rabbit called Cottontail and he belonged to Tania too. When she had made sure Frostee, the white cat, was locked up, she let the big bunny out and he hopped around enjoying his freedom, posing in among the marigolds in the garden as if he was auditioning for a Walt Disney film. Back in the hutch, he consoled himself on carrot sticks, while they all went out to the gate to see Eden's calf.

The sun was going down but the air was still warm and sweet from the heat of the day. The golden hills looked just as lovely, but nothing seemed to hold the same pleasure. How Katriona wished that she had not given her father her word to stay here a month! He would not want her to stay once he had heard Carla's version of the mess today.

'Daddy 'ere!' Jordan's shriek made her look up as Tay drove up to the gate, and all the animals in the park came racing across to get fed. Three magnificent red deer stags with spreading antlers came first, followed by the slender sleek hinds, and the big-eyed spotted fawns mingled with the goats, and further back were the geese with their strange curly feathers. Away back by the pines marched a straight line of Canadian geese in single file. The evening call of the kea came thin and clear just as the big stag threw back his head and gave a loud full-throated roar, the mating call, and then another, loud and long and vibrating. Suddenly the magic was back. She could still submerge herself in the beauty of this place and learn to love it and ignore Morgan Grant.

She met Tay as he stepped from the truck. 'Daddy 'ere.'

Tay grinned, 'You're okay, then.' He scooped Jordan up. 'Enjoy my kids?'

'I loved them.'

'I knew you would. Whisky worked, then?'

'Fine,' Katriona replied with a laugh. 'I think Amber

must have poured a full bottle into me. I feel I could jump clear over that high deer fence and skim over the plantation and fly to the mountains.'

'How about the moon? See it up there, before the sun has had time to set.' Tay gave her a searching look. 'Carla lied.'

'If you say so.'

'I say so. Why didn't you?'

Katriona shrugged her shoulders. 'What was the profit in doing that? He wanted to believe her.'

She watched Tay feed the animals and tie his dogs for the night, marvelling at the patience of the man with his children, with his stock. He was strong and sure and yet gentle. Morgan was strong and sure too, but not gentle. Morgan was cruel.

Tay walked ahead of them up the path with his bucket of barley to feed the geese and wildfowl, and Katriona waited with Tania to latch the gate. 'Peebles will get in and eat the garden if we don't shut it.'

Katriona looked at the big Hereford calf butting half-heartedly at the gate and went back to scratch his head. 'Poor Peebles, no flowers for your dinner. Have you had him long?'

'He's Eden's. I think he's about five or six months old. Daddy found the mother dying in the swamp and they went and got him in the truck. Eden will tell you where, bush camp I think.' Tania's slim little hand twined around Katriona's arm and her sweet face with its flowerlike beauty and trusting intelligent eyes smiled right into Katriona's eyes and heart. They lingered by the gate together watching the sunset change the clouds to apricot, pink and gold, and the mountains to a mysterious purple. This garden was different from the homestead garden but just as appealing with its shrubs and flowers, mignonette and honesty, marigolds and nasturtiums and cactus plants, and the rowan tree gay with huge clusters of brilliant red berries.

'We'd better go in,' Tania suggested. 'Dinner will be ready.'

Tay, freshly showered and wearing shorts and a leisure shirt, was helping Amber serve the meal, and listening to Eden talk of his school day, while Jordan and the budgie competed for the remaining air space in between. Amber was angry, her green eyes bright and fierce.

'Katriona, I thought you had more brains!'

So Tay had told her. Katriona brushed back her hair. 'Than what?'

'Than Carla. Why did you let her get away with that lie?'

'Whew! I thought you were going to take off the same way as Morgan did.'

'Me! Morgan! Me, think like that idiot man? I should hope not! I would have got the truth out of her if I'd had to beat her brains out, and I'd have enjoyed every minute of it.'

Tay grabbed his wife, silencing her with a kiss. 'It's great to be married to a quiet, gentle, loving woman, Katriona. So soothing to come home to. Tania's finished her wash, Katriona. If you like to whip in and have a quick shower, I'll send Eden out to the truck for an overnight bag of your things I picked up from Nivvy.'

'You think of everything,' Katriona said gratefully. 'This dress has pear juice stains on it and I feel I've been wearing it for a thousand years. I won't take long.'

'Don't thank me. It was all Nivvy's idea.'

Katriona enjoyed changing into an artist's smock in raw blue silk which Nivvy had chosen for her. Feeling fresh and clean still did not bring back her appetite even though Amber had prepared a good meal and a beautiful pavlova for dessert. After the children had finished and been excused to watch T.V. she sat on with Tay and Amber talking about the station but carefully avoiding any mention of the car incident. She could not bear to think of it, let alone discuss it.

'Anyone home?' Morgan called as he came up the path.

At the sound of his voice Katriona was on her feet, her back braced against the wall, her hands outstretched to Tay.

'Please don't let him in here!'

One look at her chalk-white face and her blue eyes large and dark with fright made Tay reach the door in one stride, to bar Morgan's entrance.

'Good day, Morgan. Can I help you?' Tay sounded casual.

'Yes. I want to see Katriona. May I come in? I don't usually have to ask.'

Katriona was flattened against the wall, behind the open door, out of sight of Morgan.

'Sorry, Morgan, Katriona isn't up to seeing anyone right now. We'll talk outside.' His large frame blocked the doorway.

'We'll talk inside. I want to talk to her. Get out of my way, Tay.' Morgan spoke softly, but there was a threat in his voice.

Amber whipped around and ducked under Tay's arm. 'Don't you think you've said enough to Katriona already today?'

'Keep out of my business, Amber,' Morgan snapped.

'You keep out of my house, Morgan Grant. And don't yell at me! Katriona isn't well, and she doesn't want to see you, and neither do I. You're a mean man, Morgan Grant.'

'Is she hurt?' Morgan's voice sounded concerned.

'*Is she hurt?* Oh, you mean physically—blood, bruises, broken bones kind of hurt. That's the only hurt a man like you would understand. No, she's not hurt that way, just inside, she bleeds inside, but you wouldn't understand that, would you, Morgan Grant? You get to hell out of here. Katriona is staying here tonight. In fact she'll probably stay here till Ross comes back to sort you out.'

'That will do, Amber. I'll talk to Morgan. You're too fierce darling.' Tay stepped outside, closing the door behind him.

'Sit down, Katriona. Tay won't let him come inside.' Amber pushed her into a chair. 'Would you like to join the kids in the lounge?'

Katriona hid her head in her hands and mutely shook her head.

'Sit where you are. I'll make some coffee,' Amber plugged in the electric kettle and cleared the table. Just as she poured the coffee they heard the men's voices raised in anger. It was dark now except for the moon. Amber pointed to the open bedroom door indicating that the conversation was drifting in through the window and put her finger to her lips, cautioning Katriona not to speak.

'She is not staying here with you. You see you bring her back to the homestead. Do you hear me?' Morgan shouted.

'I'm not deaf. They can probably hear you in Hanmer. And Katriona is welcome here tonight and any night she wants to stay. Taken on new responsibilities with the manager's position, have you, mate? Vetting the guests who stay on the station. Big job that, Morgan—think you're up to it? You don't own the show yet.'

There was a deep silence and Katriona tried to visualise what was happening out there in the dark. She felt guilty that these two were at each other's throats because of her, guilty also that she was eavesdropping.

'Okay. So what's your game, Tay? You decided to stir as soon as you set eyes on Katriona this morning. I could tell.'

'I've always preferred to be on the side of the underdog, and even though she's as cute as a button, and I'd guess a real gutsy little redhead, she'll need the odd friend. Well, she's got Amber and me. You said show her the station, help her learn about it, so I took her with me. It was a real pleasure. So why belly-ache about it now?'

'You want it on the line, I'll give it to you. If she stays here tonight, you're fired ... finished!'

'Katriona will spend the night with us, Morgan. Amber and I will start packing at first light. I'd rather be out of work for a year than work one more day for a bloke like you. You're wanting to visit the sins of the fathers on to the heads of the children, or in this case, you're wanting to make that poor kid suffer for the death of your parents, because you can't make her mother pay. Great stuff, Morgan. Did you ever pause to think how a mother like hers could snarl up a little kid's life? Is all the pain yours? And you'd rather believe Carla's lie than find out the truth.'

'Did Katriona say that Carla lied?'

'You don't want to know the truth, Morgan. Katriona knows that, she doesn't know why, but she knew enough not to talk to you. You can't see the wood for the trees, or I should say for the luscious bosom and buttocks.'

There was a sound of fighting, and Katriona jumped to her feet. 'Stop them, Amber, please stop them!'

'Why should I? I hope Tay belts him good and hard. He deserves it. It might make him see sense.'

'But Tay might get hurt, and it's all my fault.'

'If Tay gets hurt, so will Morgan. They're evenly matched, let them get on with it.'

Appalled, Katriona stared at her. 'You're enjoying it!'

'Every minute of it. And if Tay doesn't win, I'll beat him up myself.'

'But think, Amber, you love this place, so does Tay. Why jeopardise your position for a perfect stranger? It doesn't make sense. I'll leave right now, tonight. Morgan's right, my mother came here and caused trouble and now I've done the same. I wish I'd never come to New Zealand.'

Amber lifted her head. Her green eyes, deep and intense, met Katriona's desperate gaze. 'Don't say that, Katriona. You've been here such a short while. How can you make a judgment as to whether your visit is a good thing or a bad thing for this place? I've been here years, and I say, quite adamantly, that your coming here is the best damn thing that's happened to Evangeline for a long time. Sure, you'll stir up hidden pain and hurts which your mother left behind. But you're dead straight and honest. There's nothing false about you, both Tay and I feel that, and we're never wrong about people. You stay this month, Katriona. Believe me, this place needs honesty, large lumps of it, and you've got guts, if you'll pardon the unladylike expression. Don't

you dare go high-tailin' it back to Scotland, leaving everything to Carla. Your father needs you, Morgan needs
you ...'

'Oh, Amber, nobody needs me. I'm nothing but trouble.'
She gave a bitter laugh.

'They *need* you,' Amber said fiercely. 'Sure they don't
know how much, but that doesn't make their need any less.
And Carla ... you're just what the doctor ordered to fix
Carla. You think your mother brought trouble to Evangeline, you stick around and see what Carla does to create
trouble and you'll see that your mother was a pathetic
amateur.'

Katriona stared at Amber in blank amazement, too
dumbfounded to speak. What Amber was saying was utterly
ridiculous, yet there was no doubting her sincerity.

'Any coffee left?'

Amber was on her feet in an instant, facing Tay. She
examined him critically, her eyes narrowed. 'You're going
to have a black eye. That was careless.'

Tay roared with laughing. 'Fine welcome for a returning
warrior! Nothing but carping criticism. Yes, I'll wear a
black eye, but Morgan may have to visit his dentist. Does
that satisfy your blood-lust, wench?'

'Oh, Tay, I do love you so much,' Amber's voice was soft
and so gentle.

'I do know.' Tay smiled down at her glowing face and
brushed her cheek with his lips. 'Pour my coffee, slave,
while I wash up.'

Katriona watched, bewildered yet fascinated. They could
be losing their job because of her, yet they were treating it
like a joke. They might understand what was happening,
but Katriona could not. One question burned inside her
and she knew that she must have an answer to it.

As Tay returned from the bathroom to sit by Katriona,
Amber placed his coffee in front of him, then slipped on to
his knee, nestling into position with ease of long practice,
her head against his shoulder. 'Did you really beat him?
Did you really knock his tooth out?'

Tay sipped his coffee appreciatively. 'Good coffee, this. No, I did not beat him. I think it could better be described as a draw. Actually, it was not high drama. He hit me, I hit him, and it was all over. We realised we could both get hurt, so we called it off. He had a cut lip and said I'd loosened one of his back teeth. So you'll have to be content with that.'

Amber giggled. 'Oh, Tay, you're both so silly, you and Morgan.'

'Yes, I know ... but then we always have been. That's why we're friends.'

Katriona gasped. 'You're *still* friends?'

Tay smiled at her, 'Poor Katriona, no wonder you're all mixed up. Yes, Morgan and I are still friends. One good fight doesn't ruin a friendship. In fact it often helps one. Same as a fight doesn't break up a marriage, it clears the air and you come closer together, eh, Amber?'

'And it's such fun making up,' Amber agreed, her eyes bright.

Katriona's blue eyes reflected her troubled thoughts. 'Do you and Morgan often fight?'

'No, you couldn't say often. Once every ten years could hardly be described as a frequent occurrence ...'

Katriona stood up. 'I'm not stupid. I'm a reasonably intelligent person, yet I can't understand what went on here tonight. I'm right out of my depth, but one thing I have to know ... no, two answers I must have. Will you give me honest answers, Tay?'

'Always, Katriona. Trust me.' He became serious.

Katriona fought back the tears that threatened to overflow at the kindness in his tone. 'I heard you arguing with Morgan. He said that if I stayed here tonight, you and Amber and the children would have to leave Evangeline. Does that still stand?'

'Yes,' Tay replied.

'Even though you're still friends?'

'Because we're friends, Katriona.' Tay rubbed his chin. 'Morgan is the manager here. He laid it on the line and I accept it. You're welcome to stay here the night, more than welcome.'

'You would give up your job here, for me? You'd leave the place you love, pack up Amber and the children and all your household belongings and move out for me? You only met me today!' Katriona felt her heart was hurting too much for her to keep breathing.

Amber slipped off Tay's knee and walked over to kiss her. 'Friendship isn't something which can be measured in weight or height or length of time. It's just there. It just happens. Tay and I feel the same way. You stay here tonight. I'll leave you with Tay till I put the kids to bed.'

Katriona gripped the back of the chair with her hands, glad of its support. She felt the tears course down her cheeks. The enormity of the gift of these two people's friendship was too much for her.

She felt Tay's hands on her shoulders. 'I think you'd better sit down, Katriona. I can't have you flaking out again—I don't think we've got enough whisky left for an encore.'

'Don't laugh about it, Tay.' Katriona's voice was harsh with emotion. 'I can't carry it. It's too heavy.'

'Poor little kid, you haven't had much love in your life, if a small offer of friendship throws you like that. Have a good cry. You've been through a lot today, and it will make you feel better.'

Katriona felt his arms go round her, holding her firmly and comfortingly, and the tears flowed in a flood, soaking his shirt. She heard Amber and the children talking and moving about the room as she slowly regained control of herself, and pushed herself away from him, wiping her eyes with a large handkerchief which Amber had thrust into her hand. 'Sorry about that.'

'You're okay now,' said Tay. It was a statement, not a question.

'Yes, I'm okay now, thanks.' Katriona replied. She looked about her. Tania and Eden, freshly bathed and in pyjamas, were arguing about their books, and Jordan, clean and incredibly angelic, was in his mother's arms.

'Put him to bed, please, Tay.' Amber transferred him to his father.

Katriona watched the big fair man kiss Jordan and walk from the room. No one in the family seemed to think it very unusual that Tay should have held her in his arms while she cried all over him. They had just gone on preparing for bed.

Amber laughed at her wan look. 'Think nothing of it. Tay's good to cry on. It's his one talent. He's had years of practice with me. I think that's why I married him. He instinctively knows when the dam is going to burst, and he just holds you and lets you get on with it. I love him for it. Most guys would run a mile, or tell you to buck up, but not my Tay, he's a natural.'

'He is indeed,' Katriona said gratefully. 'And so are you, Amber. You're both beautiful.'

Amber laughed. 'Not all the time, we're not. Sometimes we're horrible. You've just seen us at our best, trying to make a good impression. You may live to regret the day you made friends with us.'

'Oh, no, I won't. *Never!*' Katriona declared with conviction.

She said goodnight to Tania and Eden, promising to come down to their school house and see them doing their correspondence lessons soon. As they left she knew she had to return to the homestead that night. These children had been born on Evangeline and she could not live with herself if they had to leave because of her.

Tay returned. 'Whew! I'd rather handle an angry stag than put Jordan to bed against his inclination!'

Katriona still had her second question. 'Tay, I still need another answer. My mother was driving the car when Ross was injured. Who else got hurt?'

Tay looked at her carefully as if trying to estimate her capacity to take punishment, then sighed. 'You've got to know, I guess, but I wish it wasn't tonight, and I wish it wasn't me having to tell you. Morgan's parents were in that car, and they were both killed.'

'How old was he?' Katriona asked harshly.

'Six years old.'

'Dear God, how terrible!' There was real anguish in her voice, and that instant she felt the agony of a little boy not even Eden's age having his parents torn from him, and understood Morgan's rage this afternoon. It must have brought it back so vividly to him. That would account for his almost uncontrollable anger.

'Were there any other children?' she asked.

'No. He was an only child.'

'That makes it so much worse. He'd be left all alone in the world. Were they happy, his parents, I mean?'

'From what I was told, yes.'

'May God forgive her, because I can't,' Katriona shouted, as she grabbed up her jacket and went to the door. 'I'm going back to the homestead, Tay. Don't involve yourself with me. Say goodnight to Amber, please. And thank you ... I ... Goodnight.'

She ran down the path and was struggling to unlatch the gate in the dark when Tay caught up with her and pushed her aside and opened it for her. 'I'll walk with you.'

'You're not trying to stop me?'

'No, I won't try and stop you.' He shut the gate. 'I'll walk you the long way home around the deer park. It will give you a little time to get things into perspective before you face Morgan. Don't forget that Carla is still there. I won't talk to you if you don't want me to, I'll just accompany you. Come this way. It's a beautiful walk in the moonlight with all the stars out. I often wander around here at night ... especially if I've got a problem. It helps me. It will help you.'

In spite of herself Katriona found herself moving with him. 'It won't help me. Nothing can help me.'

'It's very new and fresh and painful to you, but remember that it's very old to Morgan and your father. I doubt if anyone else on the station knows much except Nivvy and myself. You mustn't blame yourself, you weren't even born. Your mother did it.'

'He said I was just like my mother. He *blames* me.' The words were torn from her.

'He didn't know what he was saying. It was sort of a reflex action. He doesn't know you yet, Katriona, but he will. If you'll only give him a chance.'

'Me give him a chance? I couldn't speak to him again, never. I just couldn't.'

'You will,' Tay reassured her quietly. 'You will.'

Katriona walked, hardly seeing where she was going although the moon was bright, making the roadway white, and the sky was brilliant with stars. All she knew was that she was filled with pain, hurt beyond healing, and only barely aware of Tay walking two or three feet away from her, keeping pace with her . . . not speaking.

'Just like your mother. Just like your mother.' The words pounded and pounded into her brain like a sledgehammer driving spikes. 'A frivolous woman. A frivolous woman.' Katriona shook her head, trying to loosen the steel bands which were squeezing her head. 'A vain and stupid woman, who puts her own pleasure above the lives of others.'

The night was warm with the heat from the day still in it, but she was cold, so cold. It was as if her heart was made of ice, and instead of blood pumping through her veins it was chips of sharp-edged glass slicing and tearing at her. She clenched her teeth to keep them from chattering, and wrapped her arms across her slim body, trying to warm it.

Her mother had come here, and in her usual careless, selfish way had smashed people's lives, then fled from what she had done. No wonder she had never talked of Evangeline to Katriona. To have come here married and her husband, and orphaned a little boy, and not had the courage to stay and try to repair the damage, was beyond credibility.

She could have stayed and loved that grand man back to health, but she had left, not even knowing whether he lived or died ... not even caring. She could have stayed and given the child she was carrying to him, to give him something to live for, but she had run away ... not even wanting the child herself. She could have taken that little lost six-year-old boy and loved him ... Morgan, who would have been handsome, like Eden ... but she had run away.

Her mother was ugly, and selfish, and Morgan had judged Katriona to be the image of her mother. 'You disgust me. God help Ross Carmichael.' He had said that. Katriona moaned softly.

Tay touched her arm. 'Sit down, Katriona. Here, on this seat I built myself. You're in the picnic area now. Sit down. The seat is built strongly and will hold a great heavy weight like yourself.'

Katriona sat down, rather like a puppet which has had its strings released.

Tay kept talking. 'Look up at the stars, Katriona. What a glorious sight! See, there's the Southern Cross—no, a little this way, above that tall fir tree. See four stars in the form of a cross—concentrate. Then it has two leader stars —see them, Katriona? If you take a direct line through them, to that star on the cross, you have your bearings, whether on land or sea. Think about it, Katriona. When God made the world, he divided the light from the darkness, on the first day, and on the fourth day he made the sun, the moon and the stars. Look at them and marvel.'

Katriona looked up and found her pain easing as she took in the incredible beauty of the star-studded night, the soft wind soughing through the tall pines, and the moon spreading its light on the seats and tables, silvering the grass, and the deer by the fence, the flax bushes and small sycamore and oak trees. Slowly the chaos stilled.

'You're not alone, Katriona. You're never alone. You know that and I know that. See, those stars were put up there from the beginning of time to guide men. Navigators have used them to cross oceans and deserts. Do you think those stars were put there by accident, just flung in to make the sky pretty? Of course not. They were put there for a purpose. Everything and everyone on this earth is here for a purpose. Hang on to that thought and travel with hope.'

Katriona stared upward, filling her heart and mind with the glory of the stars, the elegant moon above the firs and the dark mountains behind them. 'Take me back to the homestead, Tay. I'm ready as I'll ever be. You travel with hope, I have none. Because for me there's nothing to hope for. If I'd grown up here my inheritance would have been the joy of being able to range free on this wonderful place, but my mother has let me inherit from her instead, just bitterness. I can understand why they're suspicious of me, and wary, but I can't understand why they wanted me here. Just to hurt me?'

'No, that's not true,' Tay contradicted her. 'Don't judge them so harshly. Give them time.'

'Morgan has judged me!' Her voice was harsh. 'Judged me and found me wanting, found I was just my mother over again. I'll stay here the month because I gave my word. I'll try very hard not to cause any trouble while I'm here, and try not to hurt anyone. That's my best offer.'

'And it's a good offer, Katriona. It won't be all bad, that's my word. Our house is your house, our family your family, you know that.'

'Thank you, Tay.' Katriona did not speak until they reached the wrought iron gate under the silver birches. 'Goodnight, Tay.'

'I'll see you to the door.' He opened the gate for her.

'Carla knew everything ... about the car ... about my mother killing Morgan's parents?'

'Yes.' Tay's voice hardened. 'She knew. She knew Morgan hates anyone to drive his car. She knew and timed your arrival at the yard at the exactly right time, because she watched from the mail box, and calculated it down to the last second.'

Katriona shuddered. She walked slowly to the pool of light streaming from the ranchslider doors. 'How she must hate me!'

Tay laughed. 'Wrong, Katriona. Think. How frightened

she must be of you.' He knocked on the door and slid it open, startling Morgan and Carla who were deep in conversation on the couch. 'One beautiful girl, signed, sealed and delivered in perfect order. All yours, Morgan. Goodnight, Katriona.'

He bent his head and kissed her cheek and whispered, 'Don't give an inch. Remember your father owns Evangeline.'

Katriona watched him leave, then walked past the two, who stood up. 'Don't disturb yourselves. I'm going straight to bed.'

'Your father rang. He was sorry to have missed you.' Carla spoke a trifle nervously.

'I'm sure you were able to explain my absence with a totally adequate and convincing lie, Carla.'

CHAPTER SEVEN

KATRIONA woke while it was still dark and hurriedly slipped into her clothes and made her way to the small building by the lane gate behind the woolshed. As she seated herself the kea called its plaintive cry, echoing the sadness Katriona felt. A stag roared and roared again in the park, and far away up in the hills another stag answered the challenge.

The sky was starting to brighten as the sun slowly dimmed the stars and outlined the mountain ridges and peaks, silhouetting the line of poplars to the east, just their slender shapes at first, but as the light strengthened each leaf and branch became delicately etched against the golden glory of the dawn sky. `

A shepherd's dog barked, and a rooster crowed, then the pure crisp morning air was filled with the song of the tuis and bellbirds in the plantation behind her. Horseshoe Hill, the twin peaks and the grey fan crater at the top changed from night-shadowed purple to a pale delicate pink, then a deeper rose shade, until suddenly the whole mountain and plateau were aflame with crimson brilliance. Katriona sat enthralled trying to capture and hold the incredible glory of the sunrise.

The big wonderful mountain had the sun to warm and colour it, while warming and lighting her was the secret knowledge she had, that she loved Morgan Grant. She had flown thousands of miles to get him out of her system, and now she knew he was a permanent fixture there. What had she lost yesterday? Nothing. What you never had, you cannot lose. The only difference between yesterday morning and this morning was knowing that she could never get close to him. Sure, it was easy to understand the hardness in him now. Her mother had done that to him, but she,

152

Katriona, would have to pay the price. He would never trust her again after yesterday. It had been a small thing to want. Just that he could like her a little and relax with her. If he had offered her his friendship that would have been a mighty gift and she would have treasured it all her life, and drawn on it in the empty years which stretched ahead. But even that was denied her. But she could still love him. In point of fact she could not stop loving him. As long as she lived she would love Morgan Grant.

'How many sunrises left?' Morgan was standing in front of her, the sun behind him hiding his expression.

Katriona glanced up automatically, not knowing that her small delicate face and shining eyes held all the awe and wonder of the morning dawn and her love for him naked and clear for him to read. But only for a second before her long lashes fanned her cheeks. She tried to control her wildly pounding heart, by staring fixedly at the majestic redwood tree by the gate as she answered in a carefully modulated voice, 'Twenty-seven.'

'And you hope they'll all be as beautiful as this morning's effort?'

'Did you see the sunrise too?' Katriona had to fight to sound casual. Her emotions threatened to choke her ... he was standing so close to her ... he was actually talking to her.

'Yes, I shared it with you. I'd been for a walk round the deer park, and was standing over there by the silos. I hesitated to come over, because I spoiled it for you yesterday.'

Katriona stared rigidly at the huge tree and wished it would not spin round like that. He had been standing there all the time. She wanted to look at him, to see what he was feeling, but dared not. Was he uplifted like her? Did he feel pity for her? Sympathy for her? Hatred for her?

'And you'll be happy to get twenty-seven more as good as this one, followed by scorching hot days?'

'Yes.' Katriona closed her eyes. She must keep her answers short, and her feelings hidden from him. *She must not look at him.* She had shared a sunrise with him. She jumped to her feet, thrusting her hands into her pockets, and deliberately turned away from him, looking towards the silos where the barley harvest was stored, and to the orchard heavy laden with fruit.

'Shows what an interest you have in the station,' Morgan said bitingly. 'You want to turn on another twenty-seven days of sunshine for your enjoyment, when we're crying out for rain. We're going through the worst drought for twenty years, stock are going short of feed, prices have fallen, and farmers are screaming for Government aid to save them going bankrupt. Several townships right here in North Canterbury are completely out of water, and have to have it all carted to them, but as long as you get a good suntan, that's all that matters!'

Katriona went pale. She did not need to look at him now. She had her answer as the angry sarcastic words slammed into her. Through her rainbow of tears she watched several brightly coloured game fowl clucking round the silos with their chicks, then looked beyond to the stags and hinds in the park. She took a deep breath. 'I'm sorry, I didn't know.'

'Oh, you didn't know,' Morgan mimicked her soft reply. 'Did you care? Do you want to know anything about Evangeline or do you just want to drift around enjoying the sunshine and scenery, and careering round the country in fast cars?'

His words cut her as if they were whiplashes. He was so unfair! She whirled round to face him, her blue eyes stormy, and her red hair flaming in the morning sunlight. 'Yes, I care. Yes, I want to know everything about this place. I want a little more than I can see, I want to know what it takes to run something as big as a sixty-three thousand-acre station. I'm not unintelligent. I want to learn. Who's going to teach me? Are you volunteering?'

He roared with laughing. 'Yes, I'll teach you. What do you want to know?'

His change of mood caught her by surprise, and her mind went blank. She must come up with one question. 'How many sheep do you have?'

'We run fourteen thousand Corriedale sheep. Next question?'

'How many cattle?'

'A thousand head of cattle, mostly Herefords. They run on the Organ Range. They'll be mustered in while you're here. Do you want to see that?'

'Yes. Will I be here long enough? How long does it take to muster a range of mountains?'

'One day. It's all done by helicopter. I drive out to bush camp with the men. Tay goes up in the chopper and shows the pilot where the cattle are and they herd them down to the flat. We drive them into the yards and draft them off, truck out those we're selling. The whole operation is completed in one day. Next question?'

Fascinated, Katriona stared at him, then realised he was waiting for her question. 'Don't you use any horses?'

'No, not for work, they've all been phased out. I still have an interest in horses—that's why I have Somali. The children have their ponies. There's Carla's hunter, she does quite a bit of Show riding.'

Katriona was not interested in what Carla did. 'You said you have a deer farm. Is that what you call the deer park?'

'No. We have nearly a thousand deer. If you want more exact figures come to the study after dinner tonight and I'll get out my diaries. You'd probably be interested to see all the newspaper clippings of the very beginning of the deer farm. The previous manager started it off on a very solid foundation so we've just followed on, but the whole thing was purely experimental at the start. Nobody really believed they could be farmed. Next question?'

'Where are the deer?'

'They run up on number one hill block. Do you want to go and see them? Actually you get a really good view of the whole station from there.'

'Yes, please, I do ... want to see them.' Katriona was appalled to hear herself stammering, but everything was happening so quickly.

'Right. I'll take you tomorrow afternoon.'

She wanted to keep him talking. 'Is that all Evangeline that way?'

'All you can see this side of the Hope. That's Bush Knob over there across the road from Horseshoe Lake, there's Kakapo Block and further down Summerdale ... see, towards Hanmer.'

'Where's Summerdale?' demanded Katriona. It seemed to her that he was just waving his hand at a lot of mountains.

He moved close to her. 'That big hill there.'

Oddly breathless, she followed his pointing finger, then protested, 'That's not a hill, that's a whole mountain.'

'My hills, your mountains, Katriona.'

Something in his voice made her look up to meet his steady grey eyes, and her vivid blue eyes were trapped and held for one timeless moment with no barrier between them, no pain, no bitterness. Colour flooded her cheeks as she became aware that she was shaking and that her shoulder was against his arm and he would know the effect he was having on her. She stepped smartly away as if she had been scorched. Morgan chuckled. She would not forgive him for that. He had leaned against her deliberately, knowing from long experience with dim-witted adoring females that she was very vulnerable.

Angrily she touched the shed she had been sitting by. 'What's this building?'

He unlatched the catch, still smiling. 'This is an overflow accommodation for the shearers. There are two bunks, water laid on, power for lights and points. Usually there's plenty of room for them all down at the cookhouse, but if we have the fencers in and a couple of extra musterers, some of them end up here. Before that it was the schoolhouse. Come in. See, there are some of the kids' posters on the wall still, and look, a bow of pine cones painted gold.

Must have been for their Christmas celebrations. Tay and I were at school here.'

Katriona wandered in, looking at the two bunks and the rest of the small room. Why, she could live here. She would be out of Morgan's way. It would be a real escape until her father came back. She only half listened to Morgan.

'Before that it was the station cookhouse. There's a man up the Lewis Pass road who would only be too happy to tell you all about this cookhouse. He owns a station now, but he started his career at Evangeline when he was only fifteen. He came here about 1917 and has a great memory. He'll tell you all about mustering on foot and when all the work was done with horses.'

He had her attention now. Hands on hips, her head thrown back to see him better, she narrowed her eyes to conceal her thoughts from him. When he was smiling as he was smiling now she would follow him to the ends of the earth if he asked her.

'He'll give you a real understanding of the history of the station. He was the cow boy here and had to milk the cows at the end of each long hard day's work. He really appreciates getting bottled milk delivered. He can tell you about carting the wool out to the Landing with horse and wagons, and driving to Culverdun in a terrible snowstorm to pick up farm machinery. He was here when the 'flu swept this country after the First World War. He could make this place come alive for you.'

'I'd love to meet him.'

'And he'd like to meet you. He's a fine old gentleman. He's a good friend of your father's. He really stuck by him when ... when ...'

As if a heavy cloud had come down between them Katriona knew he meant when her mother had run off leaving her father crippled, and himself orphaned. She had been foolish to think they could be friends. She walked swiftly out into the sunshine and stripped off her thick sweater, her slender well-proportioned body outlined against the blue sky, her unruly waves haloed by the brilliant sunshine. 'It's too hot,' she explained perfunctorily as Morgan joined her.

Morgan cleared his throat. 'Look, Katriona, I'm sorry ...'

'You're sorry! What have you got to apologise for? It was my mother who killed your parents—yes, I know all about it. I asked Tay last night. If you'd been honest with me when we met in Edinburgh I wouldn't have come here to open up old scars.'

'I know you wouldn't have come. That's why I didn't tell you the whole story.' Morgan faced her squarely.

Katriona flared angrily, 'Oh, you didn't worry about opening old scars and wounds, did you, Morgan? You just wanted to inflict a few new ones.'

Morgan's eyes were molten steel pools of fury. 'Don't be a complete idiot. Nothing was further from my thoughts.'

'Prove it. You wouldn't let me stay with Tay and Amber where I would have been happy. You were going to sack them if they kept me. You wanted me back at the homestead so you could get at me, so that Carla could make mincemeat out of me. That's your idea of a joke. Well, it's not mine. I want to stay here until my father gets back from his trip. May I have your permission to do that?'

'The hell you have! You'll stay in the homestead where you belong. I'll have no argument.'

Katriona threw her sweater on the ground. 'I'm sleeping here whether you like it or not. You haven't got any good reason to refuse me.'

'You're not. I'll switch off the power and water and rip out the bunks if that's what it takes to convince you.'

'Then I'll sleep on the floor,' Katriona threw at him furiously.

'Oh, no, you won't. Your father put you in my care. You camp down here tonight and I'll come and carry you home.'

Resentment and rage burned through Katriona, but she knew she was beaten. 'I hate you, Morgan Grant!'

'I'm not worried. I think you're a feather-brained female with an over-vivid imagination. You be in my study at eight tonight. You can have your first lesson on farm management.'

'You can be in your study at eight tonight, but you'll be all on your own. I don't want to learn anything you could teach me. I don't think you're even human!'

Morgan stepped closer. 'If you're going to have hysterics, go ahead and get it over. I'll slap your face and then we may be able to talk rationally.'

Katriona swung her arm backwards. 'I'm not going to have hysterics, and if anyone is going to have their face slapped it isn't me.'

She felt her hand caught and held firmly from behind, and turned to find Tay standing there. 'Oh, Tay!' All her anger drained away as she looked into his smiling blue eyes.

'Oh, Katriona, my friend.' Tay let her hand go and ruffled her curls. 'Morgan is too big for you to handle physically. Weight for age, he'd eat you alive. Look at my eye, a real shiner. Walked into a door. Now you wouldn't like to wear one like that, would you, Katriona? Oh, morning, Morgan. All well with you?'

'Good morning, Tay,' Morgan replied coldly.

Katriona giggled, and inched a little closer to Tay. 'May I come to dinner with you and Amber tonight, please?'

'You're always welcome, Katriona. Bed and board any time you wish.'

It was nice to have someone big for a friend, someone who was not scared of Morgan. She looked at Morgan's still dark face. 'Will you make them pack up and leave if I have a meal with them?'

'I will not.' His anger seemed to ebb away too. 'If you weren't so childish and immature you wouldn't ask such a question. Feel free to eat wherever you wish. Talk to anyone on the station. Maybe some of the men can teach you something about Evangeline, seeing you feel you can't learn anything from me. But you sleep at the homestead.'

Katriona sighed deeply as he strode away. 'I made a bit

of a mess of that, Tay, but thanks for turning up when you did.'

'When I saw you chuck your sweater on the ground I thought you were throwing in the towel and I came rushing over to put a bit of ginger into you. What did I find? You were getting ready to beat him to pulp. Come on, Katriona, you won. Smile! If I hadn't stopped you, you'd have pulled a real David and Goliath scene. You were quite safe. Morgan doesn't hit women.'

'You're wrong, Tay, I didn't win. I lost horribly. We were doing not badly and he was going to teach me all about the farm, and then it came up about Ross being hurt and away we went. It will always be that way.'

'You mean you'll always spark each other off. Yes, I think you might, but that's good. Morgan likes someone with a bit of spirit. If you'd gone all humble and apologetic you wouldn't have got anywhere with him. If you'd try to sex him up the way Carla does in her slinky, slimy, slithery way, you still wouldn't have made any impression ... she doesn't. Look, you handled it just right. When he left he was angry, bewildered and frustrated. He isn't used to being pushed backwards by a miniature female tornado. Women usually fall all over him and bore him to tears. He's not bored with you.'

In spite of Tay's cheering words Katriona felt dejected as she went towards the homestead. She could have gone on a visit to the neighbouring farm, learnt something of the economics ...

'Hi there, Katriona!'

In the middle of the yard were Gary and Jeff Travers with a flock of sheep. They both greeted her enthusiastically, explaining that they had just returned from Hope Valley Station.

Gary was still the spokesman. 'Morgan yelled for us to come back when the shearers arrived. How fares the battle with the bewitching blonde?'

'Oh, Gary, your poor car!' Katriona's hand flew to her

face as she remembered the damage she had caused. 'I'll pay for the repairs.'

'No way. Every dent in that old bomb is beautiful to me. She wears them proudly like war wounds. I've had a look and she suffered no internal injuries, so quit worrying.'

'You're sure?' Katriona was vastly relieved.

'Of course he's sure,' Jeff contributed. 'If you can think of any way we can help you get back at that one, count us in. We've got a few old scores to settle. She's a pretty mean bit of work to set you up like that.'

Katriona gasped in amazement, 'You think she set me up?'

'Of course she set you up,' Gary chimed in. 'You wouldn't have touched Morgan's car unless she'd virtually forced you to. Everyone agrees.'

'Everyone?' Katriona stared at him. 'You mean all the people on the station?'

'All the people on this station and some of the other ones. In fact everyone who knows Carla.'

'How would they know?'

'We have telephones,' Gary replied with a grin. 'And Morgan had to ring me about the car ... then some of the boys were visiting from the Lewis station. News like that travels fast ... adds a bit of variety to life.'

Katriona shook her head in wonder. 'I don't know. One moment you feel so cut off from the outside world, then you tell me this and it makes everyone seem close and interested and involved. And they all think I was set up. Incredible! I thought everyone would blame me.'

'Nobody does,' Gary assured her.

'Morgan does,' said Katriona.

'Then he must have suffered a mental block,' Gary said emphatically. 'He wasn't pleased that you'd pranged his car when he spoke to me ... which is natural, you must admit. Forget it. You come over to the yard and watch me shower the sheep.'

'You what? What will you be doing?'

Gary laughed, 'Not your sort of shower, with talc behind

the ears, and body lotion. Join us after you've had your breakfast.'

As he whistled his dogs Jeff offered with a pleasant grin, 'Nivvy says your new car is coming today. Would you let me teach you to drive, Katriona?'

Katriona bit her lip nervously. 'Oh, Jeff, I'll never be able to drive after yesterday. But thanks, anyway.'

'You're going to let Carla win? What will you say to Ross when he asks how you liked his present? Give it a go. I can teach you.'

Katriona felt really sick at the thought of getting behind the wheel of another car, but Jeff was waiting. 'Yes. I'll try.'

'We'll make a good team, believe me,' he winked, and left her standing open-mouthed. She had thought he was the quiet one!

Her heart was singing as she went up the path. She had felt so humiliated by her stupid behaviour yesterday, feeling that she had disgraced herself in everyone's eyes, but Gary said they all knew Carla was to blame. Evidently making a fool of people was something Carla did well, but she wouldn't try that on Morgan, so he'd never understand.

'Would you like a cooked breakfast?' Nivvy greeted her. 'That one's still in bed. She needs her beauty sleep, she's older than you.'

'Oh, Nivvy, you know she's quite beautiful. Not liking her doesn't change that,' Katriona laughed gaily.

'Beauty is in the eye of the beholder, and when I look at her beauty is not what I see. You didn't get hurt yesterday, did you? I wanted to rush to you, but I saw Tay get there and I knew you'd be all right.'

'There's hurt and hurt, but the bruises I got don't show.'

'I know exactly what you mean,' Nivvy stated with feeling. 'That one should have been drowned at birth ... and when I saw Morgan believing every lying word that rolled so smoothly off her tongue, I was so mad! I can tell you they got *very* skimpy servings for dinner, and I slapped the plates down in front of them. They could tell I wasn't pleased.'

Katriona gurgled with laughter, imagining Nivvy in action. Then, becoming serious, she asked, 'How do I tell Ross when he rings? How do I ever thank him for the car?'

'I've told him about the smash ... my version, and I got in ahead of her ladyship too. About thanking Ross? Are you pleased with the present?'

'Oh, Nivvy, how could you think otherwise?'

'I'm glad you think like that. Tell him so and it will warm his heart.' Nivvy beamed at Katriona with approval before answering the insistent ringing of the telephone. 'There's your opportunity now. Ross is on the blower. Take it in the study.'

As she walked through Katriona was wondering where she would get the courage to pick up the phone. Would her father also blame her for the crash? Would he be disgusted with her too? Would it bring his own accident back to him, and make him hate her?

'H-hello.'

'Ah, Katriona. I'm sorry I missed you last night. I did try. Did they tell you? Nivvy says you're happy about the car. Is that so?'

'Happy! I just don't know how to tell you how happy I am. Carla said yesterday that it was a stupidly extravagant gesture on your part. I think so too, but it's one I'll treasure for the rest of my life.'

'You don't think I'm trying to buy your affection?'

Katriona laughed with real amusement. 'You don't have to do that.'

'No, I don't. I'm just interested in your reaction. Do you feel it's your due? Me easing my guilty conscience?'

'Nothing is my due, here,' Katriona said flatly. 'As far as I'm concerned you have no reason to have a guilty conscience. You didn't even know of my existence. I'm truly delighted, not to mention overwhelmed, with your present, and I'll try to take great care of it while I'm here. Jeff Travers has offered to teach me to drive.'

'Listen to me carefully,' Ross barked. 'That's your car. If you want to pour gas over it and set it alight, that's your business. If you drive it into a gateway and bend it, you don't worry about it, or apologise for doing it, not to me, not to Morgan, not to *anyone*. Understood?'

'Understood,' Katriona repeated shakily. 'I'm sorry about damaging Morgan's car. I ...'

'I don't give a damn what happened to Morgan's car as long as you weren't hurt. He deserved what he got, lending it to Carla, and I've told him so. I must go,' he went on. 'I'm due in at a conference in two minutes. They say the Lord loves a cheerful giver, but I'll bet he's got a soft spot for those who know how to accept a gift gracefully. I'll ring tomorrow night. Take care, my girl.'

Katriona replaced the phone feeling curiously elated. Her father was pleased with her. It was a small thing, but how she longed for his approval. In a subtle way he had let her know that he was not blaming her for yesterday's catastrophe. Was that how real fathers behaved, giving their children a feeling of being sheltered and protected even when they were in the wrong? And that 'take care, girl' ... she liked that. He had said it yesterday too, as if he meant it. He was trying to take any pressure off her that might block her learning to drive, telling her that it did not matter what she did to the car. If he thought she could still learn to drive after that fright, then she would give it a real try. She felt a real rush of gratitude towards Jeff. She would take him up on that offer.

She paused for a moment on her way out of the office to gaze at the aerial photograph of the station which took up almost one wall. Her fingers longingly traced the boundary lines, hungry to take that whole vast rugged high-country station to her heart, lakes, rivers, mountains and forests. They were all spread out enticingly on the map before her, but Morgan held the key. Her father had told her that the night he left and she had stupidly thrown away her chance to know Evangeline by telling Morgan he could teach her nothing.

On her way through the kitchen she offered to give Nivvy some help with the preserving.

'No, off you go and enjoy yourself. You've little enough time. Did you enjoy your talk with Ross?'

'Oh, yes, but it was so short.' Katriona blushed, knowing she'd given away just how much it meant to her to speak with her father. 'If you don't need me I'll be off to the sheepyards. Gary said he'd let me watch him showering sheep. Do they shower sheep, Nivvy?'

'Certainly. Did you think he was kidding you? He'd do that too, but not so soon after yesterday. They were most upset to hear you'd got taken. I told you they were nice boys.'

'I won't be in for lunch, and I'm going to Amber's for dinner tonight. Is that okay with you?'

'You haven't made your peace with Morgan, then?'

'Well, he talked to me, which was unexpected, then he got mad, and I got mad, and I think I'm worse off than I was yesterday. I was just so stupid!'

'You mean yesterday? *You* were stupid? I must have been out of my tiny mind to let you go with Carla. I should have known she was up to no good. That one does no favours, there had to be an ulterior motive. I overheard her telling Ross on the phone that you wouldn't accept the car so he'd better cancel it.'

Katriona walked thoughtfully towards the sheep yards. So Carla was not content to ruin any chance of friendship between Morgan and herself, but she would drive a wedge in between Katriona and her father as well. Carefully avoiding the chance of meeting Morgan, she skirted round the woolshed and climbed over the fence to join Gary.

'Tell me what you're doing, so that I'll know at least one operation on the farm.'

Gary looked at her eager enthusiastic face. 'I'm not that crazy about the job, and I'll be doing it for the next three days at least, so I'll give it to you on an instalment plan. That way I'll get your company part of each day. Are you ready? I will now enlighten you with all the facts pertaining to ridding the sheep of their lice, ticks, or whatever else is gnawing into them from the outside and keeping them from enjoying the quality of life to which they're fully entitled.'

Katriona giggled, then became serious. 'You won't fool me, will you, Gary? I'm very ignorant and very easily fooled.'

'So I've heard.' He sounded angry. 'No, I'll give it to you straight. Later on when you're not so fragile, it may be a different story. Now, see that tractor ... I'm using it to drive the pump with this belt here ... follow ... and I'm filling this four-hundred-gallon tank with water. Now, I'm adding two pints of dip, and I'll test the shower to see it's in working order. Come over and see.' He walked to the huge circular tank and bent down, switching on a tap which sprayed jets of water up from the pipes in the bottom, then switched another lever and four overhead pipes started to revolve, sending down jets of water.

'Happy? They get sprayed for two minutes from underneath, then two minutes from the top, then I switch off, release this gate, and they're out in the yards. Seventy ewes at a time, or a hundred lambs, clean as a whistle. Right, you read that tin of dip if you really want to know what I'm killing and I'll get the sheep in.'

Katriona watched entranced as Gary whistled and worked his dogs, three at a time, one along each side of the race and one in behind the sheep with him, moving the sheep forward. It was such a clever dog, running along the sheep's backs, forcing them to move faster, and even dancing around on their backs as if on a wool carpet, when they got into the shower tank to make them crowd up, but always being fast enough to dash out just as the gate closed.

Gary switched on the water spray and moved the next pen sheep forward, closed the gate, moved the third pen one up, like a conveyor belt on an assembly line. Each time he moved a pen, he switched off either the top tap or the bottom one, or released a load of sheep. It seemed like perpetual motion to Katriona. The dogs answered the sharp whistled commands, barking, moving up and over the rails

so fluidly and smoothly, making the whole job look effort-
less and easy. Yet it couldn't be.

'Don't you ever get tired?' Katriona felt the sun beating
down on her head, making her feel dopey, but it had no
effect on the hatless Gary.

'Ask me this afternoon,' Gary answered with a grin.

'Where do you get all the sheep from?'

Gary waved towards the cookhouse end of the yards.
'See, the shepherds keep bringing them in there from the
different paddocks and blocks, then they get drafted down
there where Morgan, Tay and Jeff are working. From there
they go into the woolshed where the shearers crutch them,
and out of those portholes into the counting out pen, from
there into my race. I get last whack at them—well, almost.
Later on Morgan or Tay will put these wet wonders
through again to check for foot-rot.'

'What's foot-rot?'

Gary grinned wickedly. 'You've had today's lesson. Come
back tomorrow for part two of this enthralling serial. I'll tell
you all about the bugs that gnaw at their insides and what
we do to zap them. Of course you can stay here and admire
me all day if you like. I doubt you'd find anyone more
interesting on the whole of Evangeline, in my modest
opinion. But I do suggest you go and borrow a hat, this sun
is pretty fierce. Or else seek a bit of shade by going into the
woolshed and watching the shearers.'

'Would they mind?' asked Katriona.

'Of course not. Probably move twice as fast if you're
watching them. Be sure they see you go in, otherwise you
may hear some language unsuitable for the ears of a gently
reared lady.'

'How do you know I'm gently reared?' Katriona asked
with a laugh.

'Oh, it shows. Just go in that door, they'll notice you
immediately. Well, they'd have to be blind if they didn't.
Morgan said something to them at smoko, so they'll be
expecting you.'

'Doesn't anyone move on this station without Morgan

Grant's permission?' she demanded.

'It's always better to check with Morgan. That makes life easy. Ignore him . . . that makes life hard.'

Katriona walked towards the woolshed, luxuriating in the warmth of the sun on her bare shoulders, glad she had changed into a sun-frock. She paused a moment to watch the men drafting the sheep, watching Morgan really. Gary had said that ignoring Morgan made life hard . . . well, there was no danger that Katriona would ignore him. She couldn't. He drew her eyes wherever he walked, whenever he spoke, but that did not make life easy for her. It was as if she was a robot with some inbuilt homing device which centred on Morgan, calling her, enticing her, luring her to him.

Fighting the powerful, almost irresistible urge to walk over to where he was working and just stand beside him left her physically shaken. She wanted to be near him now, this minute. Whether he hated her, whether he was angry, meant nothing. Just to be close to him meant everything. Her longing and desire mounted until her love for him became an unendurable vibrating living fire pounding through her slender body. She would gladly trade the rest of her arid empty life for the chance to be caught and held in his arms once more before she left Evangeline.

As if becoming aware of her, Morgan straightened up, turned and looked directly at her across the empty yard, holding the drafting gate shut, the sun glinting on his dark hair and bronzed body motionless and still. Katriona's heart leapt within her as he seemed to take a half step towards her, as if answering the deep need in her.

Then he turned away and began working, and slowly her sanity returned and she lifted her eyes across the river to Horseshoe Hill, finding solace in the golden windswept tussocks and the purple-shadowed valleys. To be near him was pain and ecstasy, to be away from him was pain and desolation.

She continued on to the woolshed. Would she always feel like this? Or would the years soften and dim the memory of this month with him? And she knew the answer already. Twenty years could pass and still etched deeply in her mind, as vivid as it was this minute, would be the heat of the sun, the blue of the sky, the mountains and golden tussock hills, and herself standing in an empty yard. Standing there silently screaming her need of him, to the tall dark Morgan with his grey far-seeing eyes, and his arrogant pride, and that split second when he had almost answered her need with his ... but then had turned away.

CHAPTER EIGHT

SLOWLY the sun edged upward to herald a new day and once more Katriona witnessed the glory of another sunrise. She could hardly believe that half her allotted month had gone. Not that she had a sunrise every day. One morning she had woken up to pounding rain on the roof and it had been marvellous to watch the drought-stricken land soak up the wetness, but after only two days rain it was fine and warm again and the parched earth was beginning to turn green in places. Snow coated the mountains of the Main Divide in the distance and winter was coming close.

Her father had not returned. He was disappointed, but some urgent business had come up and he had to spend another week in the North Island. Katriona wondered what was happening today, because there seemed to be sheep and lambs everywhere, wandering through the home paddocks and the yard paddock, up and down the lane and through the plantation, calling and running around, all the way down past Tay's house and up on the hill. It must be going to be a busy day and she would enjoy that.

She had learned a lot since she had arrived. She knew all the people who worked on the station now. They often joined her on the step in the morning or later after work— all except Morgan. He gave the old schoolhouse a wide berth. The men told her stories of the station, tales of mustering, of the beginning of the deer farm, and of the wild deer and pigs which still roamed the hills. She saw them returning from shooting and hanging the carcases in the freezer, and saw the huge refrigerator trucks pull in to collect the game meat and take it through to the city.

There was the Forest Service truck going up the lane now; she gave them a cheerful wave. She knew they came each year to pick up the cones from the Scotch firs from the

Frenchman's Plantation. She knew that there was much excitement in Hanmer a week ago because someone had discovered the grave of the Countess de la Pasteur, the Frenchman's wife. So much she knew, yet so little. She even loved hearing the names of the neighbouring stations, Lochiel, Glen Hope, The Poplars, The Hossack, Island Hills, Glens of Tekoa and Molesworth and St Helen's. Some of the men had worked on these other stations and could tell her about them. She could find most of them on the map in the study.

Driving the car had been a tremendous adventure, and Jeff had been really kind to her, and it had been fun. She told her father each night about the new things that she had seen and enjoyed, and the phone calls had got longer and longer as if he enjoyed talking with her too.

Elenor Price had invited her over to the cookhouse and she had gazed in wonder at the huge pots and pans and gasped in awe as she heard the amount of food twenty-eight men could consume daily. Of course that would be a rare occasion to have so many, but it did happen. And what happened in an emergency when the cook was sick? The other wives came to the rescue, Elenor told her. When the previous manager was there his wife used to take over. Katriona enjoyed the thought of Carla being married to Morgan and having to cope with that lot. And she did not share *that* thought with her father!

Amber had taken her to visit Hope Valley Station, and that had meant wading across the Hope River which was at its lowest for years because of the drought, and Katriona had been glad to walk upstream of the horse Jordan was riding to help her keep her balance in the swiftly flowing river. They could have waited for another day when one of the men was free to take them over by Land-Rover, but it had been a real adventure and Katriona had loved it, so had Jordan. And she now knew what it was to say 'he'll do to cross the river with'. She wished she had had her father's arm or Morgan's to lean on as she stumbled over the large slippery boulders.

But apart from two trips, out to the river faces and Wallis Block, she had seen very little except for round the station homestead. Those two trips, crowded between Morgan and Tay in the truck, had been tantalising glimpses of the huge scope of the station; the land seemed to spread out ahead of the truck like a bow wave ahead of a boat. She knew that until her father came home or until she had made her peace with Morgan, she was not going to learn much more. Morgan was so mean to her. He was denying her the knowledge she longed for. Or was she denying herself, because he had taken her at her word when she had flung at him that he could teach her nothing? He had offered so much and she had thrown it back in his face. What a fool! Yet in some ways it had been wise. If she had been with him constantly she would have given herself away. Angrily she headed back to the house, wondering what all the commotion was down at the yard, men and dogs and sheep still circling.

She was surprised to see Carla up and dressed talking to Morgan and Tay by the implement shed, and as she joined them Carla pointed at her.

'Ask her if you don't believe me. Katriona—you went for a walk up the lane last night after dark, didn't you? Tell the men the route you took.'

Katriona caught Morgan's angry gaze and even Tay seemed upset. 'Don't be ridiculous, Carla!'

Katriona knew she was being accused of something but said, 'Yes, I went up the lane. I think I went through the Grandstand paddock into the Racecourse, and down through the home paddock. Has something gone wrong?'

Carla laughed in triumph. 'Told you so! I told you Katriona had wandered around like a proper townie and left all the gates open. Don't look so innocent. You just ruined two weeks work on the station and they'll take another week to sort it out. Can I do anything to help, Morgan? Cancel the trucks ... I don't mind helping.'

'I did not leave any gates open!' Katriona shouted. 'I climbed over them, that's how I know. How dare you accuse me!'

But Morgan walked away with Carla by his side, and Tay threw out his hands as he met her bewildered indignant stare.

'Ah, I'm sure you didn't, Katriona, but hell, what a mess! You've watched us muster and draft each day, and we've now got to go through the lot again. There were lambs in the lane, sale ewes in the top farm, lambs in my paddock, foot-rot ewes in the Racecourse, and the whole bloody lot are mixed up!'

'You don't believe I would do such a thing, Tay?' Katriona was appalled.

'Nope. But why the hell did you go that way of all routes to take last night? Sorry, Katriona my love. I must apologise for swearing, but this is not funny.'

The jeep went past with Morgan in it, his face stern and set, and Carla by his side looking positively smug.

Katriona sat down to her breakfast, but it was only to please Nivvy who had it all prepared for her. She toyed with her cereal, then her toast, feeling miserable and upset. She knew in her own mind that Carla had followed her around last night and left the gates open, but how did you prove something like that?

Nivvy was angry too. 'When Carla's up at daybreak there has to be a sensational reason. Don't you worry, Katriona, the truth will out about this one. I wish your father was coming home today. Sorry, I meant to tell you he'll be held up for another couple of days. Perhaps Morgan told you. He was talking to him.'

Morgan had told her nothing. Morgan had not spoken to her. Usually he at least said good morning. Katriona's heart plummeted downward. She had been counting so much on Ross's return. If she could never know Morgan, there was a little hope that she could know her father, and he would teach her about Evangeline. 'But, Nivvy, I've only got two weeks left!' she exclaimed.

'Sorry, pet. I know how you feel. Still, that's all the bad news. Good news coming up. Carla is leaving this morning.'

Katriona hardly heard her, she was so disappointed with

the news of her father. Perhaps he really didn't want to come home till she left. 'Oh, Nivvy, what shall I do?' she sighed.

'Don't know, Katriona. I wish I could help, really I do. It will be better when that one's gone. She must think she's queered your pitch sufficiently or she wouldn't be going away. How about fooling her, and making it up with Morgan? You've got two weeks. I know he's told the men he'll show you the station when he's ready.'

'Blood and sand!' It was an anguished wail. 'That's as good as telling them not to take me with them. I wondered why they'd stopped offering.'

' 'Fraid that's the reason, pet.' Nivvy looked worried as Katriona pushed her cup away and stalked out the door, then paced out to the gate and back. Katriona took no pleasure from the mountains, nor from the silver birch, nor from the roses. Anger was in every line and movement of her slender body as she came back into the room.

'Who does he think he is? He doesn't own this station. He's only the manager! Isn't he?'

Nivvy looked at her reproachfully. 'Only the manager? Come along, Katriona, you must have some idea of the responsibility that goes with a position like that. Running Evangeline isn't easy, you know. This place functions smoothly and efficiently only because Morgan has his finger on the pulse, and knows it from outside in. Why do you think your father chose him? Ross has often said to me he wouldn't have a manager on the station who didn't feel he owned the place. I mean, if the manager doesn't love the place as his own, treat the stock as his own, and handle the money as his own, then he's no good. Can't you see that? And Morgan is a good manager, especially for Evangeline ...'

'I *hate* Morgan Grant!' Katriona burst out furiously.

Nivvy laughed. 'That's the stuff! A good healthy reaction. You're Ross's daughter all right—down sometimes, but not out. Ross learned to take his knocks on the chin and come back fighting. He had some pretty bitter medicine to take on his way through. He came up the hard way. His father was a shepherd here many many years ago, but he was crippled when a horse rolled on him and the family moved up to town. But the high country was in Ross and as soon as he was old enough he left the city and got a job up the McKenzie country, milking cows, doing the vegetable garden. That's how he started, down there on the bottom rung. He was a tough young man and as soon as he got a few dogs about him and a bit of experience he moved from one big station to the next improving his position each time. He was strong and hard then, walking the tops, away at camps for weeks, days and nights on the hills, and his eyes always on Evangeline.'

Katriona stopped her pacing and was listening intently. This was the first time anyone had opened up to talk to her about Ross.

'He became head shepherd here, then five years later was offered the manager's position. He was a grand manager ... you can ask anyone around here ... he had a fantastic reputation. You know, he'd never looked at a girl ... one of those loners, mostly in the company of men and happy that way. Then he met your mother. He fell like a ton of bricks for her and she played havoc with his life. After she crippled him in the accident, I helped nurse him. Do you know what it did to a man who'd grown up in the high country to be told that he'd lie like a log in bed for the rest of his life, to be told that his wife had cleared out not waiting to hear if he would live or die? It puts iron in his soul ... that's what it does.'

Katriona saw a tear slide down Nivvy's cheek as she stared out across the yard, and Katriona knew that Nivvy loved Ross. That she had loved him for twenty years, or maybe longer.

'Did you know my father well before he met my mother?' Katriona asked softly.

'Yes, I did, pet. We were close friends. I would have been as close to him as any woman ever got, until your mother came on the scene.'

Katriona sighed. Tay would say, chalk another one up to your mother ... one more casualty of her mother's visit. Yet, Nivvy had been so very kind.

Nivvy cleared her throat after a long silence. 'Well, Ross did not lie in his bed for more than a year. He fought back. He got on his feet and kept going. He wasn't fit for the high country any more, so he moved into the business world, and he learned how to make money, and he learned it well. He made a packet. He was hard and ruthless but honest, as straight as a die. And when he'd made enough, he bought Evangeline. Not too bad for a late starter.'

There was a world of pride in her voice as she turned to face Katriona. 'Something else I'll tell you about Ross Carmichael, he was no fool, but he did make the odd mistake. And when he did, he was a big enough man to recognise what he'd done and would set about righting it. He'd go straight in, clear away the trouble and forget it. You could learn a lot from your father. You can be proud to be his daughter.'

Katriona thrust her hands deep into her jeans pockets, and walked out to the path without saying a word. She did not even notice that the yard was clear of sheep and that order had been restored. She did not wave to the men working in the sheepyards as she usually did. She just walked, not knowing where she was going, and her steps led towards the lane. Somehow the physical effort of climbing eased the pain in her heart a little. She did not notice the sunshine or hear the birds singing in the tall pines as she followed the gravel road higher and higher until she was clear above the homestead and buildings. She was blind and deaf to the beauty which surrounded her, until the sapphire blue of the tiny lake sparkling and glittering in the morning sunshine caught her eye. She turned off the lane and across the golden sun-scorched tussock until she reached the green bush-fringed edge and threw herself down.

Gold, green and blue, gold, green and blue—no wonder her father loved this countryside. She *was* proud to be his daughter ... daughter of Ross Carmichael. But she was also her mother's child ... her mother, who had wrecked so many lives in such a short time. Suddenly Katriona was crying, sobbing as if her heart would break. How could she stay here? Her very presence was a reminder to them all of what her mother had done. She could not carry that load of guilt. She would leave today. What was a broken promise? They would expect that of her. She was her mother's daughter, wasn't she? Katriona knew that she had not hurt anyone, only herself.

She had not got close enough to anyone to hurt them. Her visit here would only cost Evangeline a new farm bike. That was a small price to pay to get rid of her. The tears stopped, but she still lay there, drained and exhausted.

'Finished?' Morgan's voice brought her to her feet in one swift movement. She brushed the unruly curls from her face, knuckled her eyes to rid them of tears, straightened her yellow sun-top, dusted off her jeans and then glared at him. She thought she saw pity in his eyes and her chin went up.

'Finished what?' she demanded.

'Wallowing in self-pity. You look a right mess!'

'Thank you! That's all I need to make my day. You've got sixty-three thousand acres to manage, why pick this spot?'

He threw back his head and laughed. 'I always keep my eye out for trouble spots.'

'Meaning I'm one of them?' Katriona could feel her temper rising and tried to control it. She wanted to leave with cool dignity. She must not let him get under her skin.

'Well, I wasn't sure till I got down here. I saw you from the lane, spreadeagled on the grass, and thought you'd done yourself in 'orribly ...'

'Thought or hoped?' Katriona flashed back at him.

Morgan's grey eyes were full of laughter, 'Oh, you're not that big a problem to me, little Red. I can handle half a dozen your size before breakfast if the mood takes me.'

Katriona took a deep breath and her glance ranged across

the golden land and up to the mountains beyond. Dignity was the key word. She must not lose her temper.

'If you're looking for Tay, he won't be coming to rescue you,' Morgan told her. 'He's out on Dismal Flats. You're all on your own. Does the thought scare you? Just you and me and miles and miles of no one else.'

'You couldn't scare me, Morgan Grant, not if you practised for a hundred years. It would take a bigger man than you.' Katriona threw dignity to the winds.

'I wouldn't count on it.' There was a dangerous light in his steely grey eyes and he was smiling.

Katriona turned to run for the lane, but his arm snaked out and wrapped itself around her like a steel band, pulling her closer and closer to him. Then he held her to him, ignoring her struggles. Gently with his free hand he stroked her hair, smoothing the flame-coloured curls, his hand then tracing the sweet outline of her face. Katriona stopped struggling, and was still ... she could not get away from him, she had neither the strength nor the desire to try. Her heart was pounding, sending the blood coursing through her veins, and the bittersweet knowledge was that while he was only teasing her, she was getting what she longed for ... just once to be held in his arms ... just one kiss before she left Evangeline for ever. And she knew he was going to kiss her ... *oh, how she knew!*

'Relax, little Red, you're going to enjoy this, and so am I,' he spoke very softly.

She resisted for a moment, then looked up at him, her blue eyes twin pools of burning, longing love. She was leaving today. Did it matter what he read in her eyes? It had never mattered, she had never had a chance. 'Why not?' Her voice was husky.

She felt his arm slacken as she relaxed and her arms wound around his neck as she moved closer into his embrace and heard his heart beating in tune with her own, closing her eyes as he cupped her chin in his hand, tilting her face upwards to his. Before his lips brushed hers lightly she knew that she would remember this moment till the day she died, the warmth of his hard body against hers, the touch of his hands on her body, and then as his lips moved softly against hers, tauntingly teasing, suddenly something beyond his control or hers exploded between them. Her whole being responded to the urgency of his demand and her world of blue, green and gold was blotted out in a rapture undreamed of, as she gave free expression to the flame of love and desire which she had held in since the first day she met him.

At last it was over ... her one kiss, the kiss that would carry her for the rest of her life and never let her love another man. As Morgan put her gently away from him, her eyes flicked open to surprise the same awe and wonder in his eyes that she was feeling.

Before he could speak she said quickly, 'I'm leaving to-day, Morgan. I hope you'll arrange for someone to take me to Christchurch.' She turned and walked slowly up the hillside towards the truck.

He was at the door before her, barring her way. 'Why have you decided to leave today, Katriona?'

'Because I must leave *now*,' she answered flatly, her eyes downcast.

'Because I kissed you?' he mocked softly.

Katriona flung her head up to glare at him. 'Certainly not! What's a kiss?'

He was smiling down at her as he leaned against the truck door. 'I thought that was a very special kiss.'

'Nothing special about it. I always kiss like that,' she replied with seeming nonchalance while she knew she lied.

'Lucky Donald!'

Colour flamed in her cheeks. She had never kissed Donald like that. Morgan laughed. He knew she had not. 'Why lucky Donald? There are other men in the world besides yourself and Donald.'

'Oh, a very experienced young woman of the world.' His eyes sparkled with disbelief. 'You could have fooled me. Your eyes are shining, your lips are soft and sweet, and your whole expression so vulnerable and innocent ...'

'I've been kissed like that hundreds of times!' Katriona shouted.

'Then you were right. There's nothing I can teach you.' There was no mistaking his meaning.

'I want to go home. Turn that truck around and take me back so I can pack, and stop annoying me. You've had your fun.'

'It was fun, wasn't it, Katriona? I mean, even for an expert such as yourself, you would have to admit it was a very satisfying kiss. Answer me, Katriona.'

She wanted to slap that teasing smile right off his face, but she did not dare come too close. 'All right, I enjoyed it. Satisfied?'

'Very.'

She turned away to look at the lake. He was playing with her as a cat plays with a mouse. She would refuse to answer him again. Her lips set mutinously.

'Oh, definitely your best profile, little Red.'

She turned her back to him, then heard him move and swung around defensively. 'You keep away from me, Morgan!'

He laughed. 'I was only opening the door for you. Hop in.'

She edged past him nervously and pulled the door shut with a vigorous slam. She sat as far away from him as she could, thankful he was driving the International truck which had such a nice wide seat, wide enough to get four people in. That left a good distance between them.

Morgan sat relaxed in the sunshine, making no move to start the truck.

'I want to go home,' Katriona demanded a little desperately.

'Why? Why the sudden decision to leave Evangeline?'

'I'm homesick. Donald needs me . . . I need him.'

'Make up your mind.'

'Both!' Katriona shouted wildly.

'And that's a good enough reason to break your promise to your father?' His voice was harshly critical.

'It's what he'll expect of me. He won't be surprised. Even you can't pretend to be surprised. I'm that image of my mother you carry in your mind, aren't I? A vain, frivolous woman who puts her pleasure before other people's lives. Well, nothing I can do can wipe out what she did. You think I'm a liar. You think I drift around in a dream, leaving gates open and making a lot of work for you. You believe Carla. You won't even show me the station. My father can't even bear to come home while I'm here. So I'm leaving. I wish I'd never come in the first place!'

His face darkened ominously. 'Before you go, allow me to straighten you out on a few points. First of all, I did not believe Carla. Carla always lies. I asked for your side of the story, but you refused to say anything. Next, your father is so excited about having a daughter that his business colleagues haven't had to buy themselves cigars since you arrived. He planned a surprise party for you this Saturday night. All his friends from the neighbouring stations are coming to Evangeline for a barbecue to meet his daughter. But you won't be here. And finally, if I ever said you were the image of your mother, I retract the statement absolutely. I would elaborate further, but I'd be wasting my time.'

Morgan started the engine and moved off, heading away from the homestead.

'Turn around! Where are you taking me?' Katriona yelled.

'I'm kidnapping you. Sit back and enjoy it.'

'I'm getting out here,' she retorted.

'I wouldn't if I were you. I'll set the dogs on you.'

'You would too!'

'I would.'

Katriona sat back in her seat, ramrod-stiff, her arms folded across her chest and her eyes closed tightly.

'You won't see much of the station that way.'

'I don't want to see the station,' she muttered from between gritted teeth.

'If you don't open your eyes this instant, I'll stop the truck and kiss you.'

Her eyes flew open wide.

'That's better. I'm taking you up the hill to see the deer before you leave.'

'That's not a hill, that's a mountain. Your hills are my mountains,' Katriona remarked stubbornly.

'I'll let you keep this one for a mountain because it's marked Mount Kakapo on the map, and we're going right to the top, you and I.'

'I don't want to. Not with you. Not in this truck.' She did not want to learn any more about Evangeline. She just wanted to get away from all the pain and bitterness that her coming had stirred up. Even Nivvy. . . .

'The truck is quite safe. It's a four-wheel-drive vehicle. You don't want to go on the tops with me? Why ever not? Don't you think I could teach you anything?'

'I'd rather go with Tay. Tay is kind,' Katriona threw at him.

'Tay is soft. Not your kind of man, Katriona. You need a firm hand to keep you in order. I don't think Donald is big enough for the job, if you want my advice.'

'I don't want *anything* from you.'

Morgan stopped in front of a huge cyclone gate. 'The truck is safe. I'm not. Don't push me too far or you may regret it. Here's the keys, open the gates.'

'Why do you padlock so many gates?' she asked.

'Each of those deer is worth about a thousand dollars, and there'll always be thieves and poachers where you've got valuable stock. Out!'

She sat still for one moment openly defying him, but his expression was enigmatic, and his tanned body taut and muscles tense. *He was not safe.* He was like a panther poised to spring on its prey.

Shakily she grabbed the keys and battled to unlock the six-foot-high double gates. Morgan drove the truck through while she had another struggle to close them. She could hear him whistling his dog Flame and wanted to watch to see if he was as good as Tay, but she had to close the stubborn lock first.

'It helps if you remove the key, then the padlock will close.' He sounded impatient.

He could have told her when she left the truck instead of making her feel an idiot. She turned to tell him so, then stood staring. Down the hill came deer, red deer, hundreds and hundreds of them, with Flame working them as if they were sheep. Down through the tussock they came, some running, some walking, some leaping over the low mata-gouri shrubs, or jumping from rocky ledges, incredibly graceful, stags and hinds, slender legs, pointed ears and big eyes.

Katriona's eyes were enormous as she watched the moving mass come closer and closer and then pour through the gate a little along from her, and watched entranced as they fanned out across the next block, moving in lines higher and higher up the golden tussocks till they disappeared from her sight in hidden gullies and valleys. Twenty or thirty stood just through the gateway, their heads turned, their ears pricked watching her curiously.

'Oh, I've never seen anything more wonderful! That was fine ... just fine.' Her small attractive features were lit up with the excitement and wonder of seeing such a sight, and her voice was soft and breathless. 'Oh, thank you for making me come. Thank you for showing me your deer.'

'Get in the truck,' Morgan barked almost harshly, ignoring her delight and putting Flame back in the crate.

Katriona climbed in the truck, feeling as if he had thrown a bucket of cold water over her. He wasn't bringing her here to show her something lovely. He was doing it as a duty. She was leaving and he was doing what her father said he must. It hurt. She moved along the seat a little closer to him to show that she wanted to be friendly, to show that she wanted to share the joy of this remarkable experience with him.

He appeared remote and uninterested, not even noticing her shy gesture. He kept his eyes on the unbelievably steep winding track which twisted and curled tortuously round the side of the mountain, taking them always higher. Perhaps he was wise, Katriona sighed. Of course he had to watch the road. There was no room for error. But he could have said *something*. They had once shared a sunrise. The thought brought a lump to her throat. She would never see another sun rise over Evangeline. She was leaving today.

Fiercely she tried to keep her gaze on the tiny thread of road ahead of them, but as if drawn by a magnet her eyes turned back to him. This was the last time she would see him. She noted his thick dark hair, his firm jawline and chin, his superbly handsome profile, his deeply tanned skin which highlighted the whiteness of his teeth, his mouth ... There she stopped. She touched her own mouth with the back of her hand as her thoughts winged backwards to the lake. *Oh, Morgan Grant, I love you.* So intense was the feeling burning her up that she longed to reach out and touch his cheek, or smooth his dark hair, or even move closer so that her shoulder touched his ... She thrust her hands into her jeans pockets to keep them under control, and shut her eyes tight to blot out his image, but as if chiselled into her mind she could see him more clearly with her eyes closed.

'Open the gate,' he ordered.

'Are we at the top?'

'Almost. Just through this gate and up to the summit. You didn't say you were scared of heights,' he commented dryly.

'I'm not scared of heights,' Katriona protested.

'Then why did you shut your eyes?'

She felt her cheeks flame as she jumped from the truck. He had been fully aware of her every movement coming up the mountainside ... her every thought. Her small gesture of friendship, her studying his face in detail and her longing to touch him. Angrily she pulled the gate open. Touch him? She would rather touch a cobra! Morgan was as creepy as a snake and twice as deadly.

He drove the truck through, steering it closer and closer

to her, trying to make her give ground. She knew he had plenty of room, that he was trying to frighten her, just teasing. She would not move an inch. He could run over her if he liked. The mudguard almost touched her, and she glared at him, finding only his derisive smile and mischief-lit grey eyes laughing at her.

She ignored him.

He stopped the truck before it was completely through the gateway which prevented her from shutting the gate.

She looked at him disapprovingly, and he laughed out loud at her. But he did not move the truck. He was waiting for her to ask him. He would wait a long time. She knew he was watching her in the rear vision mirror, so she leaned against the gate, her free hand on her hip in an apparently relaxed attitude. Relaxed she was not. She would like to murder him. Ignoring her for days on end, then yelling at her, then kissing her as if he almost meant it, then not talking to her coming up the mountain and worse, much worse, knowing why she closed her eyes.

Giving him a very superior glance she said scathingly, 'You're being very childish and immature.'

He threw back his head and laughed, a great shout of laughter.

That did it. Katriona abandoned the gate and using the rear wheel climbed up on the deck of the truck and started to let his team of dogs out one by one. As she loosed the second dog Morgan jerked the truck forward and she flattened out on the deck. She wasn't hurt, but she was smiling as she dropped nimbly to the ground and closed the gate. She sat smiling as he caught his dogs.

She faced him squarely as he got into the truck, the light of battle still in her eyes and a victor's smile on her lips. She had beaten him. Oh, such a tiny victory, but sweet nonetheless.

He leaned over and ruffled her hair. 'You're Ross Carmichael's daughter all right. The man who marries you won't be looking for the quiet life.'

'You're indeed fortunate that it's not your problem.'

'I am indeed.' Morgan whistled cheerfully as he drove along the fence line towards the summit. 'If you climb out and walk to that rock you'll get a good view.'

She stepped up by the rock at the very top of the mountain and took a deep breath, and held it ... unable to let it go, caught by the soul-stirring beauty of the scene before her, the blue sky, the mountains and the valleys, the fields, lakes, rivers spread out unendingly before her incredulous eyes. A sudden gust of wind swept her off balance and she grabbed for the rock and let her breath out slowly as she straightened up. This time she braced herself against the force of the wind.

This time she remembered to keep breathing, but quietly, slowly, as awestruck her gaze wandered from craggy mountain peak to the floor of the valley below. Away to her right in the distance, where the blue Hope River flowed between the towering bluffs and open country, she could see a tiny miniature village. It was Hanmer, miles and miles away, just a dot on the landscape. Strange, she should be feeling small standing there on the summit, but she did not. She somehow felt grand and mighty as if she was almost part of it all.

The wind kept pushing her ... but she even felt at one with the wild wind too, as it swept up over the glorious golden tussock, moving it in fantastic flowing waves rippling over her and past her. The song of the wind became the song in her heart, superb music, divine music. The thrilling harmony swelled and swelled filling her mind, body and soul until she could hardly bear the aching sweetness of it all.

'See the deer on the other ridge.' Morgan spoke softly.

She looked across at the hill near her and saw several deer standing among the small rocks and matagouri bushes, and their hill too was a golden flowing mass of yellow tussock. They stood alert and wary, yet not frightened, then delicately picked their way around the shoulder of the hill and out of sight.

Morgan spoke again. 'Do you like what you see?'

'Oh, it's beautiful ... beautiful ... I haven't the words ...
It's like being on the roof of the world. This must be what
God saw when he made the world and was pleased that it
was excellent in every way.'

'Yes, you can feel that up here.'

She turned to look at him to see if he was sincere, and
was reassured. His grey eyes regarded her intently as if he
knew how she felt, and had felt that way too. There was no
anger in his eyes, and no laughter, just a quiet understanding and something else. She rested her slim hand on
his arm lightly as her mind tried to accept what she saw
there, a tenderness, a kindness and a lovingness that was
too much for her. She turned away from that look, not
ready to believe it.

The panorama stretched out before her again and she felt
she could stand there for ever and ever and still not see it
all.

This must be why Nivvy said high-country men were
different. She had only been on the tops this once, and she
felt lifted up with the joy of it, yet at peace with herself.
Men of the mountains came here again and again and refreshed themselves, looking down on the valleys and level
with the mountains. No wonder they walked tall, and with
confidence, and had those steady far-seeing eyes.

She knew that Morgan was holding her hand, that he
had carried it to his lips, that he was holding it against his
rough cheek. Wordlessly she looked at him and accepted the
love he offered and gave him her heart in return.

Now the wind sighed softly over the tussock caressing it
lightly, moving it tenderly into intricate and exotic patterns.
Katriona felt attuned to the mood of the wind as it touched
her cheeks and lovingly swept through her hair and over
her body. The music in her heart changed also to such a
hauntingly exquisite air that she felt the tears running down
her face.

Morgan Grant loved her. She would never leave Evangeline. She could live here ... she could range free ...
because Morgan Grant loved her.

Just as suddenly the wind changed again, growing stronger and stronger, buffeting her body, forcing her back a step, then another step, even though she braced herself against it. The wind blew wilder and wilder, the song louder and louder, exulting, pulsating and vibrant, reaching an impassioned crescendo as it swept her backwards into Morgan's waiting arms. Even the wind knew they belonged together, was Katriona's last clear thought as Morgan's lips claimed hers again.

When at last he lifted his head she asked with stricken eyes, 'Morgan, what about Carla? She told me you were going to marry her.'

'I told you Carla always lies,' Morgan said with an outrageous grin.

The sheer enormity of the statement took her breath away. She knew he had said something the same down by the lake, but she had been so upset that she had not believed him. Only his anger had registered. And he had said she wasn't like her mother at all. She sat beside him in a sunlit, sheltered hollow on the mountain, fascinated that she fitted as comfortably against him as Amber had to Tay ... it did not take years. Shyly she tilted her face towards his, wordlessly demanding another kiss, and his response was satisfyingly swift and ardent. Would she ever get used to the wonder of it?

'My mother ...' she began, then faltered, needing time to put her thoughts into words. 'Morgan, I think I can understand my mother a little ... It suddenly came to me that I could have reacted much the same as her in similar circumstances ...'

'Never.' His reply was emphatic.

Katriona persisted. 'I could have killed someone that day I drove your Mustang. Say I'd driven into Tay and Amber and killed them, or you'd attempted to save them and I'd run over you and crippled you ... could I have stayed and faced the consequences? I doubt it.'

'You would have,' Morgan assured her. 'But I agree with you. Perhaps your mother has carried more blame than she should have. It was something Ross said after you had that upset. He asked who was really to blame—the driver? The person who gave the incompetent driver permission to drive? I thought about it a lot, applying it to the accident when my parents were killed. Should Ross have let your mother drive? Who knows, who cares? That accident wrecked their lives, but I have no intention of allowing it to wreck ours.'

'Thank you for sharing those thoughts with me, Morgan,' Katriona said quietly. 'It's lifted that awful load of guilt I was almost staggering under. As for who cares . . . I do. My mother crippled Ross physically, but she did worse to herself. She became an emotional cripple, unable to face herself and what she did, unable to love anyone, always running away. I can feel sorry for her . . . I would like to love her, if she'll let me. She had all this and she lost it.'

'You're in danger of doing the same thing unless you devote some of your time and love to me this very instant,' Morgan told her flatly.

'How much time? How much love?' Katriona teased, then laughing, 'You can have all my love, all my time, for all my life . . . Does that satisfy you?'

'It will do for starters,' Morgan replied, gathering her into his embrace.

Harlequin Romances

The books that let you escape
into the wonderful world of romance!
Trips to exotic places... interesting
plots... meeting memorable people...
the excitement of love.... These are
integral parts of Harlequin Romances –
the heartwarming novels read by
women everywhere.

Many early issues are now available.
Choose from this great selection!

Choose from this list of Harlequin Romance editions.*

*Some of these book were originally published under different titles.